Reckoning at Windermere

Preview

: Who Is Lady Phillips?

The year was 1872, and Eleanor Phillips was the undisputed matriarch of Windermere Hall. Born into wealth and married into power, she had spent her life upholding the family name, ensuring that the Phillips legacy remained untarnished. Windermere Hall, with its grand halls and sprawling grounds, was more than a home— it was a fortress of tradition, its walls whispering with centuries of secrets.

But Eleanor's reign was not without tragedy. Her husband, Phillip, had died young, leaving her to raise their son, Edward, alone. She poured her heart into him, molding him into what she believed was the perfect heir. Yet, Edward had other plans. Wild and reckless, he squandered the family's fortune on gambling, liquor, and women, dragging the Phillips name through the mud.

Eleanor begged, pleaded, and eventually threatened, but Edward was beyond her control. One fateful evening, after a night of debauchery,

Edward returned to Windermere Hall, drunk and enraged. Their argument echoed through the house, the culmination of years of frustration and disappointment.

"You've ruined us!" Eleanor shouted, her voice trembling with fury. "You've destroyed everything your father and I built!"

"Built?" Edward spat, his words slurred. "You mean controlled. Suffocated. Maybe I don't want to live under your rules anymore, Mother."

That night, Edward stormed out of Windermere Hall, never to return. Days later, Eleanor received word of his death—an accident, they said. But deep down, she knew the truth. Edward's recklessness had caught up with him, and she blamed herself.

The Turning Point

Grief consumed Eleanor. She withdrew from society, sealing herself within Windermere Hall. The staff whispered of strange occurrences—the sound of footsteps in empty hallways, the flickering of lights, and Eleanor's long conversations with no one. Her grief turned to obsession, and her obsession turned to judgment.

"If Edward was weak," she muttered to herself, "then perhaps I was too soft. People must be held accountable for their choices. Only then can they truly understand the weight of their actions."

Eleanor's fixation grew darker. Servants who lied, stole, or disobeyed found themselves dismissed in disgrace. Guests who overstayed their welcome spoke of strange visions and unexplainable cold. Windermere Hall became a place of whispers and fear.

Eleanor Phillips died in 1889, but her presence never left the Hall. Her restless spirit became its guardian and its judge, holding all who entered accountable for their sins. Over the years, her legend grew—Lady Phillips, the spectral judge of Windermere Hall, who saw through every lie and exposed every hidden truth.

Modern day 2025

Chapter 1: The Arrival

Jamie Phillips reclined in the back seat of the sleek black Bentley as it wound its way up the long gravel driveway to Windermere Hall. The car's plush leather interior smelled of new money—a smell Jamie adored. His manicured fingers scrolled lazily through his phone, checking the latest on his Sydney penthouse renovation, while the imposing silhouette of the Hall grew larger in the distance.

"God, what a monstrosity," Jamie muttered, flicking his sunglasses down from his carefully coiffed blond hair. "It looks like something out of a horror film. Grandfather must've been completely senile to keep this dump."

The driver said nothing, accustomed to Jamie's tirades. Jamie had made his disdain for "all things old" painfully clear from the moment he'd landed at Heathrow, huffing about the estate's remote location and outdated grandeur. To Jamie, Windermere Hall wasn't a piece of family history;

it was a ticket to a lifestyle upgrade. Sell the Hall. Pocket the millions. Jet back to Sydney.

He stretched his legs as the car came to a halt. "Finally," he groaned. His designer loafers crunched against the gravel as he stepped out, dressed in linen trousers and a crisp white shirt unbuttoned just enough to reveal a hint of his gym-sculpted chest.

Before him stood the Hall: a sprawling gothic masterpiece of turrets, ivy-draped stone, and stained-glass windows that glinted in the late afternoon sun. Its silence was unnerving, the kind of silence that seemed to press in on you. Jamie didn't notice—or care.

"Jamie!" A shrill voice cut through the air, and he turned to see his childhood nanny, Mrs. Whitaker, hurrying out from the grand front doors. She was thinner than he remembered, her gray hair swept into a tight bun, her face lined with concern. "It's been years—"

"Whitaker," Jamie interrupted, holding up a hand. "Spare me the reunion, yeah? I've only got a few days, and I'm here to sort things out, not reminisce." He breezed past her, not waiting for a reply.

Inside, the Hall was an overwhelming clash of grandeur and decay. The high ceilings, adorned with intricate plasterwork, seemed to mock him with their opulence. Dust clung to the air, the scent of aging wood and faded memories seeping into his nostrils.

"Charming," he muttered, running a finger along a mahogany banister and grimacing at the dust it collected. "This place is a health hazard."

Mrs. Whitaker trailed behind him, wringing her hands. "Your grandfather loved this Hall. It's been in the family for generations. He would want you to—"

"To do exactly what I please," Jamie snapped, spinning on his heel. "Which means selling it to the highest bidder and moving on. This," he gestured dramatically at the cavernous hall, "is not my scene."

Whitaker pursed her lips, her eyes narrowing ever so slightly. "And the staff? The groundskeepers? What will happen to them?"

"Not my problem," Jamie said with a dismissive shrug. "They can find other jobs. I'm not running a charity."

He stalked off, leaving Mrs. Whitaker to glare at his back, her face a storm of emotions she dared not voice.

In the drawing room, Jamie found a brandy decanter waiting for him, along with a stack of legal documents. He poured himself a generous glass, his movements as smooth and calculated as the man himself.

"Here's to the Phillips legacy," he said mockingly, raising the glass to the dimly lit room. "Soon to be someone else's problem."

As he sipped, a chill passed through the room, causing him to glance toward the large portrait above the fireplace. Lady Phillips stared down at him, her eyes fierce even in oil paint.

"Creepy old bat," Jamie muttered, but something about the way her eyes seemed to follow him made him down the rest of his drink in one gulp.

Chapter 2:

The Invitation

Jamie lounged on the leather sofa in Windermere Hall's cavernous drawing room, his feet propped on a priceless ottoman that had seen better days. A half-empty glass of brandy rested precariously on the armrest as he tapped away on his phone. His face lit up with the glow of the screen, but his expression radiated only boredom.

"Right," he muttered to himself, scrolling through his contact list. "Time to liven this place up."

He selected the group chat titled "The Sydney Elite" and began typing.

Jamie Phillips: *Guess who inherited an actual castle? Party at my haunted mansion this weekend. Bring your wildest selves. You're not ready for this.*

A slew of responses came pouring in almost instantly.

Lucy: *Haunted? Ugh, Jamie, are you serious? You KNOW I'm terrified of ghosts.*

Dane: *Haunted mansion? Say no more. I'll bring the champagne and something... stronger.*
Olivia: *Will there be a hot tub? No ghosts better show up while I'm in it.* **Nate:** *Sounds like a vibe. What's the dress code? Gothic chic?*

Jamie smirked, savoring their reactions. He fired off a quick reply.
Jamie Phillips: *Dress code? As little as possible.*

Tossing his phone aside, he leaned back and stared up at the chandelier above. It swayed ever so slightly, though there wasn't a breeze to be felt. Jamie frowned but quickly brushed it off, attributing it to the Hall's "ancient foundations." He grabbed his glass and drained the last of his brandy.

Later That Week

The Hall was transformed. The dusty, echoing rooms were now a chaotic blend of neon lights, blasting music, and the rhythmic thrum of baselines. Jamie had spared no expense, hiring a team to spruce up the space just enough to make it tolerable for his guests. The great hall was now a makeshift nightclub, complete with a DJ booth, champagne fountains, and an outrageous display of excess.

The partygoers began to trickle in, one by one, their laughter echoing through the Hall. They were exactly as Jamie expected—dressed to impress, exuding confidence, and oozing wealth. Lucy, draped in a designer dress that hugged her curves, sashayed in first, followed by Nate, who had gone for a tuxedo with a deliberately undone bowtie to maintain his "casual charm."

"Jamie!" Lucy squealed, throwing her arms around him. "This place is insane. Like... Downton Abbey meets *The Shining*. I love it."

Jamie grinned, the compliment feeding his ego. "Wait until you see the rest. There's a pool on the east wing, bedrooms bigger than most people's apartments, and enough booze to keep us going for a week."

"And ghosts?" Nate teased, grabbing a glass of champagne from a passing waiter. "Are we expecting any spooky visitors tonight?"

Jamie smirked. "Only if they can handle the open bar."

As the night wore on, the party descended into chaos—exactly as Jamie had hoped. The guests sprawled across the Hall, filling every room with laughter, music, and debauchery. Couples disappeared into darkened corners, and the air grew heavy with the mix of perfume, alcohol, and something more illicit.

In the grand dining hall, a group of Jamie's friends gathered around the long oak table, which had been hastily converted into a surface for drinking games. The once-regal chairs were now draped with jackets, discarded shoes, and champagne stained napkins.

Jamie, at the head of the table, raised his glass. "To new money," he declared, his voice slurring slightly. "And to proving my family's obsession with tradition was total bollocks. Cheers to doing things my way."

"Cheers!" the group chorused, their laughter echoing through the Hall.

Unseen by the revelers, a shift occurred in the atmosphere. The shadows in the corners of the room seemed to grow darker, denser. The chandelier above the table began to tremble again, the crystals tinkling faintly. None of the guests noticed, too absorbed in their revelry.

In the portrait above the fireplace, Lady Phillips seemed to glower more fiercely. The brushstrokes of her painted face appeared sharper, her eyes more piercing. If anyone had looked closely, they might have sworn her lips curled into a faint, disapproving smirk.

From somewhere deep within the Hall, a low creak echoed—a sound like an ancient door groaning on its hinges. It was faint, almost imperceptible beneath the noise of the party, but it carried a chill that seemed to ripple through the walls.

Jamie stood to refill his drink when the lights in the Hall flickered once, twice, then plunged the entire space into darkness. A collective gasp rose from the crowd.

"Relax!" Jamie called out, his voice dripping with confidence despite the unease prickling at the back of his neck. "It's just the wiring. This place is older than God."

The guests chuckled nervously, their laughter faltering when the sound of footsteps echoed from somewhere above. Slow, deliberate footsteps that grew louder and louder, as if someone—or something—was descending the grand staircase.

Jamie's grin wavered as a chill passed through the air. For the first time, a flicker of doubt crossed his mind. "Who's there?" he shouted, his voice cutting through the silence.

No answer. Just the echo of those relentless footsteps.

Chapter 3:

The Playboy's Playground

The party was in full swing, and Jamie Phillips was the undisputed king of it all. He leaned back in a velvet armchair, a tumbler of Scotch in one hand and a cigar in the other. His tailored shirt was unbuttoned to his navel now, revealing his bronzed chest—a testament to his years of lounging under the Sydney sun rather than any actual hard work.

The grand drawing room was filled with the hum of drunken laughter, the clinking of glasses, and the low thrum of house music that someone had inexplicably decided to play through a Bluetooth speaker perched on a priceless antique credenza. Jamie didn't care. The Hall might have been his family's pride and joy, but to him, it was just a backdrop for his ego.

He raised his glass to no one in particular, slurring slightly. "Ladies!" he called out, his voice cutting through the noise. "Why are we wasting such… delicious scenery?" His gaze lingered on Lucy, her curves accentuated by a figure-hugging red dress. She rolled her eyes but smirked nonetheless. "You, Lucy, are the Mona Lisa of Sydney. No, scratch that—you're better. She's flat. You're... not."

A ripple of laughter ran through the room, but it was laced with unease. Jamie's compliments always felt more like veiled challenges, daring the recipient to argue or blush.

Lucy raised her glass with a fake smile. "You're too kind, Jamie."

"Kind? No." Jamie smirked, draining his drink. "Honest. And honesty deserves a reward." He snapped his fingers at a waiter—one of the poor locals he'd hired for the weekend. "Another round, mate. And make it quick. Thirsty guests are unhappy guests."

The waiter, red-faced, scurried off to fetch the bottle of vintage champagne Jamie had insisted on serving. Jamie watched him go, then turned back to his friends, grinning. "See that? Efficiency. You've got to crack the whip, people. No one respects you if you're soft."

Olivia, lounging nearby in an emerald-green slip dress, raised an eyebrow. "You've got some nerve, Jamie. Cracking whips and calling women Mona Lisas. Careful, or you'll lose your adoring public."

Jamie leaned forward, his grin widening. "Lose them? Impossible. You're all here because you love me." His eyes raked over Olivia in a way that made her shift uncomfortably. "And let's be honest, Liv, that dress? You're wearing it for me."

Olivia narrowed her eyes, taking a slow sip of her martini. "Maybe I just like looking good."

"For me," Jamie repeated, leaning back smugly. "Don't fight it, darling. It's only natural. Money and power are irresistible, and lucky for you lot, I've got both."

The group exchanged glances, their laughter growing more forced. Dane, seated on the arm of a couch, snorted and muttered, "Careful, Jamie. You're about to choke on that ego of yours."

Jamie waved him off. "Ego? Please. If I had one, I wouldn't be throwing this party, would I? This is for you." He motioned broadly at the room, the Hall, and everything in it. "Consider it my farewell gift before I ship this pile of bricks off to the highest bidder."

Jamie was already onto his fourth drink of the night, and it showed. His charm had curdled into arrogance, his laughter into sharp-edged taunts. He prowled the room, dropping casual insults disguised as jokes.

"Nate, mate, you're still single, aren't you? Shocking, really, with that face. You've got all the charm of a wet sock."

"Nate's fine," Lucy cut in, trying to steer the conversation away from Jamie's barbs.

"Fine?" Jamie laughed loudly, throwing his arm around her shoulders. "No, Lucy, *you're* fine. Nate's just... average." He gestured toward her drink. "Careful with that champagne, darling. Wouldn't want to ruin that dress—or those curves."

Lucy shrugged him off with a strained smile, but Jamie barely noticed. He was already moving on, demanding attention from the next guest, refilling his glass as if the alcohol were fuel for his ego.

Unbeknownst to Jamie, his antics were not going unnoticed. From the shadows of the drawing room, Lady Phillips watched. Her painted visage glared down from the portrait above the fireplace, her eyes flickering with a malevolent light. The room seemed to hum with an invisible energy, the chandeliers trembling faintly as if disturbed by an unseen wind.

As Jamie threw his head back in laughter, a subtle creak echoed through the room. It was the sound of something shifting—something old, something angry.

Jamie turned to the waiter, who had returned with a tray of champagne flutes. He snatched one, spilling some of the golden liquid onto the antique Persian rug. "About time," he snapped. "I could've died of thirst."

The waiter opened his mouth to respond, but before he could, the lights flickered violently, plunging the room into momentary darkness. A scream rang out, sharp and panicked, as the champagne flute slipped from Jamie's hand and shattered on the floor.

When the lights came back on, the group froze. One of the chandeliers was swinging wildly, and the portrait of Lady Phillips had tilted, her face now turned slightly... as though she was looking directly at Jamie.

"Bloody hell," Jamie muttered, his bravado slipping for the first time. "Who's playing games?"

The room fell deathly silent, save for the faint sound of footsteps echoing somewhere above them.

Chapter 4:

The Devil in the Details

Jamie strutted through the grand dining hall, his glass of Scotch sloshing dangerously close to the rim as he leaned over the shoulder of one of his female guests. Bella, curvy and glowing in a gold sequined dress, glanced up at him with a mixture of amusement and mild discomfort.

"Bella, Bella," Jamie drawled, swirling his drink and giving her a smirk that he likely thought was irresistible. "You've got the kind of figure that would make a statue jealous. How is it you're still single, darling?"

Bella chuckled nervously, brushing a strand of dark hair from her face. "Maybe I just haven't found the right guy."

"Right guy? Nonsense." Jamie placed his glass on the table and leaned closer, his cologne an overwhelming cloud of expensive spice. "What you need is a man who knows how to appreciate a woman like you. Curves in all the right places, a laugh like champagne bubbles—Bella, you're a masterpiece. Shame if no one's enjoying the art." Across the table, Olivia raised her martini glass with an exaggerated roll of her eyes. "Jamie, have you ever considered taking a vow of silence?"

He turned to her with a grin, undeterred. "Olivia, my dear, jealousy doesn't suit you. But since you're asking..." He leaned across the table toward her, his voice lowering conspiratorially. "I'd break a vow of silence for you. That little green number you're wearing? Like a forest fire— hot and dangerous."

The group groaned, a mix of laughter and exasperation, but Jamie simply shrugged and straightened up, basking in the attention. He was the sun, and everyone else in the room were mere planets, drawn into his orbit whether they liked it or not.

Jamie raised his glass, commanding silence with the sheer force of his arrogance. "Ladies, gentlemen, and all you lucky souls in between," he began, gesturing grandly to the room. "Welcome to Windemere Hall—the last hurrah of this godforsaken mausoleum before I sell it off and make better use of the family fortune."

A cheer rose from the crowd, though a few of the guests exchanged uneasy glances. Jamie's disdain for his inheritance was as glaring as the sequins on Bella's dress.

"I know what you're all thinking," Jamie continued, his grin widening. "Jamie Phillips, finally embracing his roots. Finally getting serious about family legacy." He laughed, a sound that was more of a bark. "Wrong! This place is just a bank account in stone. And when it's sold, I'll be swimming in enough cash to fund all our wildest dreams."

"You mean *your* wildest dreams," Olivia quipped, taking a pointed sip of her martini.

"Darling," Jamie shot back, "my dreams are your dreams. Trust me, you'll thank me when we're all sipping cocktails on a yacht in the Mediterranean."

Lucy leaned against the table, her crimson lips curling into a sly smile. "What about the ghost stories, Jamie? Aren't you worried the buyers will run screaming when they hear about Lady Phillips?"

Jamie waved a dismissive hand. "Lady Phillips? Please. She was just some miserable old hag who couldn't handle anyone having fun. If anything, I'd say I'm her reincarnation." He raised his glass again. "To being fabulously judgmental!"

As the group laughed and drank, the chandelier above their heads gave another ominous creak.

This time, Bella noticed. She glanced upward, her brow furrowing slightly.

"Did anyone else hear that?" she asked.

"Hear what?" Jamie replied, pouring himself another drink.

"That... noise. From the chandelier."

Jamie followed her gaze and shrugged. "Relax, darling. This place is older than half the country. It's bound to groan a little. Like me when I'm surrounded by beautiful women who keep their distance." He gave her a wink that made her wince internally.

As the night wore on, the revelry only grew more debauched. A drinking game had begun in the parlor, and Jamie was at the center of it all. Each guest took turns revealing embarrassing secrets or daring one another to push the limits of their inhibitions. Jamie thrived on the chaos, egging them on with a wicked gleam in his eye.

"Alright, Bella," Jamie said, leaning forward with a predatory grin. "Truth or dare?"

Bella hesitated, the room's collective gaze landing on her. "Dare," she said finally, lifting her chin defiantly.

"Bold. I like that," Jamie said, pouring her another glass of champagne. "I dare you to kiss the most attractive person in this room."

The room erupted in cheers and catcalls as Bella's cheeks flushed. She glanced around nervously before leaning over to plant a quick kiss on Lucy's cheek, much to the group's delight.

"Safe choice," Jamie teased, his grin widening. "But I think we all know the real answer was me."

Lucy rolled her eyes. "Oh, give it a rest, Jamie. You've got all the charm of a used car salesman."

Jamie laughed, tipping his drink toward her. "And yet, here you all are. Proof that I'm irresistible."

Unseen by the revelers, the shadows in the corners of the room began to shift. The chandeliers swayed gently, their crystals tinkling like faint whispers. Lady Phillips' portrait loomed above the fireplace, her painted gaze sharper than ever. The air grew colder, though no one seemed to notice in their drunken haze.

As Jamie downed yet another drink, a soft creak echoed through the room. It was faint, almost imperceptible, but enough to make Bella glance toward the door.

"What was that?" she asked.

Jamie snorted. "Relax, darling. It's probably the wind. Or the ghost of my disapproving grandmother come to scold us for having too much fun."

Bella shivered. "It didn't sound like the wind."

"Then let's hope it's the ghost," Jamie said, raising his glass with a devilish grin. "I'd love to see what she thinks of this party."

Before anyone could respond, the heavy oak door to the parlor slammed shut with a deafening crack. The group froze, their laughter dying in their throats. Jamie stared at the door, his cocky grin faltering.

"Alright," he said, his voice tinged with irritation. "Who's the joker?"

No one answered. The room was deathly silent, save for the faint sound of footsteps echoing down the hall.

Chapter 5:

The First Warning

The group sat frozen, their eyes darting toward the door that had slammed shut with such force it sent vibrations through the room. The music playing faintly in the background suddenly cut off, leaving a thick silence in its wake. For a moment, no one spoke. Even Jamie, so full of swagger and bravado moments before, seemed unsure of himself.

"Alright, very funny," he said finally, his voice carrying a forced nonchalance. "Whoever's trying to spook us, you've had your laugh. Now open the door."

No one moved. Bella hugged herself, glancing around nervously. "I don't like this, Jamie. That wasn't just the wind."

Jamie rolled his eyes, already tiring of the theatrics. "Of course it wasn't the wind, Bella. It's an old house. The door probably swung shut because of a draft."

"Drafts don't sound like footsteps," Olivia muttered, staring at the dark hallway visible through the tall windows.

Jamie turned to her, his irritation flaring. "Oh, come on, Liv. Don't tell me you're buying into this ghost nonsense. I thought you were smarter than that."

"Smarter than staying in a house where the doors slam shut by themselves?" she shot back. "Definitely."

Before Jamie could retort, the chandelier above the table gave a loud groan. It wasn't subtle this time. The heavy fixture swung slightly, its crystals clinking together in a dissonant melody. Everyone at the table stared upward, their breath catching.

Lucy was the first to speak, her voice shaky. "Jamie, what's going on? That thing's bolted to the ceiling. It shouldn't be moving."

Jamie drained his glass and stood, his movements deliberately slow and exaggerated as though trying to convince the others—and himself—that nothing was wrong. "Alright, alright, enough of this. I'll prove to you there's nothing creepy about this place."

He strode to the fireplace, where Lady Phillips' portrait loomed over the room, her piercing gaze seeming to follow his every step. Jamie stared up at the painting, smirking. "If there's a ghost here, let's see it. Go on, Grandma. Show us what you've got."

"Jamie!" Bella gasped, horrified. "Don't provoke it!"

"Provoke what? A painting?" Jamie laughed, but it sounded hollow, even to him. "Lady Phillips wouldn't dare mess with me. I'm her bloodline. Her precious legacy."

In the shadows, the air grew colder. The flickering candlelight dimmed, and a low creak echoed through the room, like ancient wood straining under invisible weight. The group shifted uneasily, their earlier bravado fading fast. Olivia rubbed her arms, muttering under her breath, "I knew this was a bad idea."

The silence was broken by a loud crash. Everyone jumped, their eyes darting toward the far end of the room, where a champagne flute lay shattered on the floor. No one had touched it. No one was standing near it.

Bella's hand flew to her mouth. "Jamie... this isn't funny anymore."

Jamie hesitated, his smirk faltering. He turned back to the group, his tone sharp. "Alright, which one of you is messing with me?"

No one responded. Lucy, visibly pale, pointed toward the painting. "Jamie... look."

He turned back to the portrait, his stomach twisting despite himself. At first glance, nothing seemed different. Lady Phillips' stern expression remained frozen in the oil paint, her eyes locked forward. But then he saw it. The necklace. The painted pearl necklace around her throat had been askew moments before, a small detail Jamie had mocked earlier in the evening. Now, it hung perfectly straight, as though someone—or something—had fixed it.

Jamie blinked, his chest tightening. "Alright," he muttered. "That's... weird."

"Weird?" Olivia snapped. "Jamie, her necklace just moved! Are you seriously not freaked out?"

"It's just a coincidence," Jamie said, though his voice lacked conviction. "The paint probably... shifted or something."

"Paint doesn't shift," Dane said flatly. "Unless the ghost did it."

Jamie glared at him. "Enough. I'm not letting some family myth ruin my night."

As if in response to his words, the chandelier above the table groaned loudly, its crystals jingling violently. The group scrambled away from the table as the heavy fixture began to sway more and more, until with a deafening crack, one of the crystal arms broke free and shattered on the table below. Shards flew everywhere, narrowly missing Bella, who screamed and stumbled back into Jamie's arms.

"Jesus Christ!" she gasped, clutching his arm. "Jamie, we need to leave. Now."

But Jamie, ever the skeptic, brushed her off and stepped forward, inspecting the damage with a frown. "It's just an old chandelier," he said, though his voice was noticeably quieter now. "Nothing supernatural about it."

"Are you kidding?" Lucy snapped. "That thing could've killed someone!"

Jamie shrugged. "It didn't, though. See? Everyone's fine."

"Not for long, if we stay here," Olivia muttered, glancing nervously around the room. The shadows seemed darker now, the cold more biting.

Jamie picked up his drink and took a long sip, as though the alcohol could shield him from the growing unease. "Alright, everyone, let's stop acting like children. It's a stormy night in a creaky old house. Things go bump in the night. Big deal." "And the painting?" Lucy asked, her voice trembling. "The necklace? The footsteps?"

Jamie rolled his eyes. "Coincidence. That's all it is."

Before anyone could argue further, a low, guttural laugh echoed through the room. It was soft at first, almost indistinguishable from the wind outside, but it grew louder, more distinct. A deep, hollow sound that sent shivers racing down their spines.

Jamie froze, his drink halfway to his lips. The laughter seemed to come from everywhere and nowhere all at once. Slowly, he turned to the portrait of Lady Phillips. Her painted eyes stared back at him, colder and more piercing than ever. And this time, her lips seemed to have curled into a faint, mocking smile.

Chapter 6:

The Cracks Begin to Show

The laughter faded as quickly as it had begun, leaving a suffocating silence in its wake. No one dared speak. Jamie, standing closest to the portrait, stared at Lady Phillips' face, his smirk now a thin line of uncertainty. His pulse hammered against his temples, but he refused to let the fear seep into his expression.

"It's... probably the wind," Jamie muttered, though his voice carried none of its usual bravado.

"The wind doesn't laugh," Bella whispered, clutching Lucy's arm. "And paintings don't smile."

Olivia, standing near the windows, glanced toward the dark corridor beyond. "I'm not staying here," she said firmly. "Jamie, I don't care how much booze you've got or how many jokes you crack. Something's *wrong* with this place."

"Olivia, for God's sake—"

"No," she cut him off, her voice sharp. "You don't get to dismiss this, Jamie. You dragged us all here to show off your inheritance, and now look what's happening! You can't explain it, and you're too arrogant to admit you're scared."

Jamie's jaw tightened, but before he could respond, the candles on the dining table flickered violently, their flames shrinking and growing as if caught in an invisible gust of wind. The room grew colder still, the chill biting at their skin.

Dane, usually the loudest in any room, took a step back, his bravado slipping. "Okay, this isn't funny anymore. Jamie, what's going on?"

"I don't know!" Jamie snapped, his frustration boiling over. "Do you think I planned this? What, you think I hired some magician to make candles flicker and chandeliers fall? Don't be ridiculous."

As Jamie spoke, a loud, echoing thud reverberated through the Hall, like the sound of a heavy door slamming shut in the distance. The group collectively jumped, their eyes darting toward the doorway. The sound came again— closer this time—and with it, the unmistakable creak of footsteps.

Slow. Deliberate. Heavy.

"Is someone else in the house?" Bella asked, her voice barely above a whisper.

Jamie hesitated, his mind racing. "Of course not. I had the staff leave hours ago."

"Then who's walking around?" Lucy demanded.

"Let me handle this," Jamie said, grabbing a candelabra from the table and heading toward the door.

"Jamie, don't," Olivia said, reaching for his arm. "Don't be an idiot."

Jamie yanked his arm free, his pride too wounded to back down now. "You lot can cower here if you want. I'm going to prove there's nothing to be afraid of."

He stepped into the corridor, the flickering candlelight casting long, eerie shadows on the walls. The footsteps continued, echoing from somewhere above. Jamie tilted his head, his grip tightening on the candelabra.

"Hello?" he called out, his voice ringing through the empty Hall. "Whoever's up there, you're trespassing. Show yourself!"

Silence. Then, faintly, a whisper—soft and indistinct, like the rustle of fabric or a breath against his ear. Jamie froze, his eyes darting around the corridor.

"What the—"

Before he could finish, the door to the dining room slammed shut behind him, sealing him in the dark corridor. He spun around, his heart pounding. "Alright, who did that? Open the door!"

On the other side, the group stared at the closed door in stunned silence. Bella stepped toward it, her hand trembling as she reached for the handle. "Jamie?" she called out.

There was no response.

Jamie stood in the corridor, his chest heaving. He wasn't about to admit it, but the fear was creeping in now, cold and insidious. He turned back toward the staircase, the source of the footsteps. The grand staircase loomed before him, its ornate banisters twisting upward into the darkened upper floors.

"Alright," he muttered to himself, gripping the candelabra like a weapon. "If there's someone up there, I'll bloody find them."

The first step creaked loudly under his weight, echoing in the oppressive silence. Then the second. Each step felt heavier than the last, as if the Hall itself were resisting him. When he reached the top, he paused, peering down the long corridor lined with doors. The air was colder here, and the candle's flame sputtered as though it might go out.

"Hello?" he called again, his voice steadier than he felt.

From the far end of the corridor came a faint sound. It was like a hum, a tune carried by the air, soft and haunting. Jamie squinted into the darkness, his skin crawling. The melody grew louder, more distinct, until he could recognize it: a lullaby. One he hadn't heard since he was a child, sung to him by his mother when he visited the Hall.

"Who's there?" he demanded, his voice cracking. The tune stopped abruptly, replaced by silence so thick it pressed against his ears.

He took a step forward, and then another, the floorboards creaking beneath him. As he approached the door at the end of the corridor, he noticed it was slightly ajar. A faint glow seeped through the crack, as if someone were holding a candle inside.

Jamie reached out, his hand shaking as he pushed the door open. The room beyond was empty, save for an old rocking chair that sat in the center, its back to him. It was moving slowly, creaking with every sway. On the floor beside it lay a child's doll, its porcelain face cracked, one eye missing.

Jamie swallowed hard, his pulse racing. "This... this isn't real," he muttered, stepping into the room. "It's just a trick. Someone's messing with me."

The rocking chair stopped suddenly, as though the occupant had risen. Jamie froze, his breath catching in his throat. Then the chair turned, slowly, the sound of wood scraping against wood filling the room.

No one was there.

Jamie backed away, his heart hammering. As he turned to leave, the door slammed shut behind him with a deafening bang. He whirled around, the candelabra shaking in his hands. On the wall beside him, words began to appear, scrawled in jagged, blackened letters as if burned into the plaster.

YOU WILL PAY FOR YOUR SINS.

Jamie stumbled back, his scream echoing through the empty Hall.

Chapter 7 The Cracks in the Group

The dining room felt stifling in its silence as the group stared at the door Jamie had disappeared through. Bella was still gripping Lucy's arm, her nails digging into the fabric of her dress. Olivia paced by the windows, muttering to herself, while Dane poured another glass of champagne, his hand shaking slightly.

"This is insane," Olivia finally snapped, breaking the tense quiet. "What the hell is going on here?"

"It's just Jamie being Jamie," Dane said, though his voice lacked conviction. "He probably slammed the door himself to freak us out."

"You really think he's capable of this?" Lucy gestured at the room. "The flickering lights, the chandelier almost killing us, the laughter—none of this is normal."

"Maybe it's some sort of elaborate prank," Dane suggested. "You know how Jamie loves being the center of attention. Wouldn't surprise me if he hired a team of actors or something."

Bella turned on him, her eyes wide with fear. "A prank? Are you serious? Did you hear that laugh? That wasn't human, Dane."

"She's right," Olivia said, her pacing growing more frantic. "And what about the portrait? We all saw it. The necklace moved. Are you saying Jamie painted that himself while we weren't looking?"

Dane shrugged, clearly uncomfortable. "I'm just saying there's probably a logical explanation."

"Logical?" Olivia barked out a humorless laugh. "Dane, we're in a haunted house, and Jamie just wandered into God-knows-where after shouting at his dead grandmother's ghost. Logical left the building hours ago."

Bella sank into a chair, burying her face in her hands. "I told him not to provoke her. Why does he always have to push things too far?"

"Because he's Jamie," Lucy said bitterly. "He's spent his entire life thinking nothing can touch him. Money, charm, his family name—it's all he's ever needed to get by. But this..." She trailed off, her eyes darting to the closed door. "This is different."

Olivia stopped pacing, crossing her arms. "We need to leave. Now. Jamie can find his own way out of this mess."

"Leave him here?" Bella asked, horrified. "We can't just abandon him."

"Why not?" Olivia snapped. "He's the reason we're here. He's the one who mocked Lady Phillips and treated this whole place like his personal playground. If anyone deserves to be left behind, it's him."

"Olivia, that's harsh," Lucy said, though her voice wavered. "We don't know what's happening to him."

"Exactly!" Olivia threw up her hands. "We don't know what's happening to him. And I, for one, don't want to stick around long enough to find out."

Before anyone could argue further, the candles on the table flickered wildly, their flames shrinking to almost nothing before surging back with an unnatural brightness. Bella let out a small scream, clutching at Lucy as the temperature in the room seemed to plummet. Frost began to creep across the edges of the windows, the glass cracking slightly under the sudden chill.

"What the hell is happening?" Dane whispered, his voice trembling.

The door to the dining room rattled violently, as though someone—or something—were trying to force it open. The group froze, their eyes locked on the handle as it turned slowly, almost mockingly.

"Jamie?" Bella called out, her voice shaking.

The door swung open with a loud creak, revealing only the darkened corridor beyond. No sign of Jamie. No sign of anyone.

"Okay, I'm out," Olivia said, grabbing her coat from the back of her chair. "I'm not waiting around to be the next victim of whatever this is."

"Wait," Lucy said, grabbing her arm. "You can't just leave."

"Watch me," Olivia snapped, yanking her arm free. She stormed toward the door, but as soon as she stepped into the corridor, the sound of footsteps echoed from above. Slow, deliberate, and uncomfortably close.

She froze, her breath catching in her throat. "Hello?" she called, her voice unsteady. The footsteps stopped, followed by a low, guttural whisper that sent shivers racing down her spine.

Olivia turned back to the group, her face pale. "We're not alone," she said, her voice barely above a whisper.

Dane downed his champagne in one gulp, setting the glass down with a trembling hand. "Alright, this is officially too much. If Jamie's not back in five minutes, I'm out of here."

"And go where?" Lucy shot back. "We're in the middle of nowhere. It's pitch black outside, and there's a storm coming in. Do you really think wandering around the countryside is safer than staying here?"

"Safer than being trapped in this house," Dane said. "At least out there, we're not at the mercy of whatever's haunting this place."

Bella glanced toward the door, her voice small. "What if it follows us?"

"What are you talking about?" Dane asked, frowning.

"The ghost. Or spirit, or whatever it is," Bella said, shivering. "What if it's tied to us now? What if leaving won't make it stop?"

"Great," Olivia muttered. "So we're damned if we stay, and damned if we go."

"Stop it!" Lucy snapped, her voice rising. "Arguing isn't going to help. We need to stick together, or this thing will pick us off one by one."

"You don't know that," Dane said, his tone sharp. "You don't know anything. None of us do."

"Then why don't you come up with a plan?" Lucy challenged. "Since you're so sure of yourself."

Before Dane could respond, a loud crash echoed from upstairs, followed by the unmistakable sound of Jamie screaming. It wasn't a cry of pain or anger—it was pure, unadulterated terror.

The group froze, their eyes locked on the ceiling above.

"What the hell was that?" Bella whispered.

"Jamie," Lucy said, her face pale. "Something's happening to him."

"No kidding," Dane muttered, his voice shaking. "The question is, do we go after him, or do we get the hell out of here?"

Before anyone could answer, the door to the dining room slammed shut again, this time with such force that the candles on the table went out, plunging the room into darkness.

In the pitch black, Bella let out a strangled sob. "I don't want to die here," she whispered.

From somewhere in the shadows, a voice answered. But it wasn't Jamie's. It was cold, hollow, and laced with malice.

"You won't leave here alive."

Chapter 8:

Jamie's Descent

Jamie's scream echoed through the dark halls of Windermere Hall, but no one came. He stumbled backward from the burning words on the wall— *YOU WILL PAY FOR YOUR SINS*—his breath coming in ragged gasps. The candelabra in his hand shook so violently that wax splattered onto the floor, forming pale droplets against the dark wood.

"This... this isn't real," he whispered, trying to steady himself. But the words on the wall didn't vanish, and the air in the room felt charged, as if it were alive.

The rocking chair behind him creaked again, slowly swaying in an invisible breeze. Jamie turned toward it, his pulse pounding in his ears. The doll that had been lying at its base was gone. His throat tightened as his eyes scanned the room.

"Alright, very funny," he called out, his voice cracking. "You've made your point, whoever you are. You can stop now."

No answer.

The shadows seemed to shift, swirling at the edges of his vision. Every instinct screamed at him to run, but his pride refused to let him bolt like some terrified child. Instead, he forced his legs to move toward the door, the candelabra lighting his path in flickering, uneven bursts.

The corridor was colder now, the chill biting into his skin. Jamie moved quickly, his footsteps echoing against the walls. He needed to get back to the others, needed to prove to himself that he wasn't losing his grip.

But the Hall seemed determined to stop him.

As he reached the top of the staircase, the air thickened, slowing his movements. It felt as though he were wading through water, every step an effort. The whispers began again, faint and indistinct, like a chorus of voices just out of reach. Jamie's grip on the candelabra tightened, his knuckles white.

"Shut up," he muttered, his voice shaking. "Shut up, shut up, shut up!"

The whispers didn't stop. Instead, they grew louder, swirling around him like a storm. His name was among them now, spoken in tones that ranged from mocking to mournful. *Jamie... Jamie... Jamie...*

"Leave me alone!" he shouted, his voice echoing through the Hall.

The whispers stopped abruptly, replaced by a heavy silence. Jamie's chest heaved as he stood frozen at the top of the stairs, his eyes darting around. Then, from somewhere behind him, a familiar voice called out.

"Jamie?"

He spun around, his heart leaping. "Bella?" he called, his voice tinged with desperation. "Is that you?"

There was no reply, but a faint light appeared at the end of the corridor. It was warm and inviting, a stark contrast to the oppressive darkness surrounding him. Jamie hesitated, his mind racing. Every rational part of him screamed that it was a trap, but the part of him that clung to hope—hope that he wasn't alone—propelled him forward.

The light led him to a door he didn't recognize, one he was certain hadn't been there before. It was slightly ajar, and the warm glow spilled out into the corridor. Jamie pushed the door open cautiously, the candelabra held high.

The room was small and sparsely furnished, with a single chair in the center and a fire crackling in the hearth. Sitting in the chair was a figure—a woman with her back to him, her posture stiff and unmoving.

Jamie swallowed hard, his throat dry. "Hello?"

The figure didn't respond. Slowly, he stepped closer, the candelabra casting long shadows across the room. His footsteps seemed unnaturally loud against the creaking floorboards.

As he neared the chair, his breath caught in his throat. The woman's hair was dark and neatly pinned, her dress a faded gray that looked like it belonged in another century. And though he couldn't see her face, he felt her presence— heavy, suffocating.

"Lady Phillips?" he whispered, the words barely audible.

The figure moved. Slowly, agonizingly, her head tilted to the side, as though she'd heard him. Then she began to rise from the chair, her movements jerky and unnatural, like a puppet on strings.

Jamie stumbled back, his pulse roaring in his ears. "Stay away!" he shouted, the candelabra shaking in his hands.

The figure turned to face him, and Jamie's scream tore through the room.

The door slammed shut behind him, trapping him inside. His scream echoed once more, then cut off abruptly, leaving the room in total silence. Outside, the faint sound of footsteps moved down the corridor, heading toward the group downstairs.

Chapter 9:

Panic Rising

Downstairs, the remaining group huddled together in the dining room, their earlier arguments now drowned out by the oppressive silence that filled the Hall. Bella sat clutching a throw pillow, her face pale, while Olivia paced the length of the room, muttering to herself. Lucy tried to stay composed, though her trembling hands betrayed her. Dane, on his third glass of whiskey, leaned against the wall, attempting to mask his unease with forced nonchalance.

"Jamie's been gone too long," Bella whispered, breaking the silence. "Something's happened to him."

"Yeah, he probably scared himself stupid and ran into a wall," Dane muttered, but his words lacked conviction.

"Stop it!" Olivia snapped, her pacing coming to an abrupt halt. "This isn't some prank. We've all felt it—this place isn't normal. Jamie might be a jackass, but he doesn't just disappear."

Lucy leaned forward, her voice steady but low. "Olivia's right. Something's wrong here. The lights, the portrait, the... laughter. None of this is a coincidence."

"I'm not sticking around to find out what's next," Olivia said, grabbing her coat. "Jamie wanted to play ghost hunter, fine. He's on his own. I'm leaving."

Bella's voice wavered. "But the storm—"

"I don't care about the storm!" Olivia shouted, her eyes wild. "I'll take my chances out there before I stay one more second in this cursed house."

Dane scoffed, though his grip on his whiskey glass tightened. "You're just gonna wander through the woods in the middle of the night?
Brilliant plan, Liv."

"At least I'm doing something," Olivia shot back. "You're just standing there pretending like none of this is real."

"I'm not pretending anything!" Dane snapped, his voice rising. "I just don't think panicking is going to help anyone."

"Panicking?" Olivia laughed bitterly. "This isn't panicking, Dane. This is survival."

As the argument heated up, Lucy stood and held up her hands. "Enough! Fighting isn't going to solve anything. We need to stay together."

Olivia shook her head. "Together? Are you serious? This house is picking us off one by one. I'm not waiting around to be next."

Before Lucy could respond, the lights flickered again, casting the room into momentary darkness. Bella let out a strangled gasp, clutching at the table for support. When the lights came back on, the room felt colder, and the air was thick with tension.

"Did anyone hear that?" Bella whispered, her voice barely audible.

"Hear what?" Dane asked, though his voice wavered.

"That... that sound. Like footsteps. Upstairs."

The group fell silent, their ears straining. And then they heard it—a soft, deliberate creak, as though someone were moving down the staircase. The sound was faint but unmistakable, each step slow and purposeful.

"Jamie?" Lucy called out, her voice trembling.

The footsteps stopped.

Olivia's eyes darted toward the dining room door. "We can't just sit here. If that's Jamie, he might need our help."

"And if it's not Jamie?" Dane asked, his face pale.

"Then we run," Olivia said simply. "But we can't stay in this room forever."

The group hesitated, their fear palpable. Finally, Lucy nodded. "She's right. We need to see what's going on."

Reluctantly, they made their way to the dining room door, their steps hesitant. Dane opened it slowly, peering out into the corridor. The flickering candlelight cast long, shifting shadows on the walls, but the hallway appeared empty.

"Nothing," Dane said, his voice barely above a whisper.

"Then where's Jamie?" Bella asked, clutching Lucy's arm.

A faint creak echoed from the staircase, drawing their attention. As they turned toward the sound, they saw him.

Jamie stood at the foot of the stairs, his face pale and expression blank. His shirt was torn, and his hair hung limply over his forehead. He swayed slightly, as though he were struggling to stay upright.

"Jamie!" Bella cried, rushing toward him. But as she reached him, he raised a hand, stopping her in her tracks.

"Don't," he said, his voice hollow and unfamiliar. His eyes, once full of arrogance and bravado, now held only emptiness.

"What happened to you?" Lucy asked, her voice shaking.

Jamie didn't answer. Instead, he looked past them, his gaze fixed on the dining room. "She's here," he said softly.

"Who?" Olivia demanded. "Who's here?"

Jamie's lips curled into a faint, bitter smile. "You'll see."

Before anyone could react, the chandelier above the hallway began to sway violently, its crystals clinking together in a dissonant symphony. The temperature plummeted, and the group huddled together as an oppressive presence filled the air.

Jamie turned to face them, his eyes dark and lifeless. "She's not done yet."

From somewhere behind them, a cold, hollow voice echoed through the Hall. "No one leaves Windermere ."

Chapter 10:

Jamie's Fate

The oppressive silence that followed Jamie's haunting declaration left the group frozen in place. Bella clutched Lucy's arm, her nails digging into the fabric, while Olivia took a step back, her hands trembling. Dane, still holding his whiskey glass, seemed to have forgotten how to breathe.

Jamie stood motionless, his expression blank but his eyes burning with something none of them could place—fear, sorrow, or perhaps resignation. When he spoke again, his voice was low, almost unrecognizable.

"She doesn't want you to leave."

"Jamie," Lucy said, taking a hesitant step toward him. "What... what happened to you?"

He didn't answer immediately. Instead, he raised a hand and ran it through his disheveled hair, his fingers shaking. "She showed me," he muttered, almost to himself.

"Showed you what?" Olivia demanded, her voice sharp. "Stop talking in riddles, Jamie!"

Jamie's eyes flicked up to meet hers, and for a moment, there was a flicker of the old Jamie—the arrogant playboy who thought the world revolved around him. But it was gone in an instant, replaced by something hollow and broken.

"My sins," he said simply.

"She showed me everything," Jamie continued, his voice trembling. "Every selfish thing I've ever done. Every person I've used. Every time I laughed while someone else cried. I saw it all, as if I were living it again. But this time... I could feel their pain."

"What the hell are you talking about?" Dane asked, though his voice was unsteady.

Jamie laughed bitterly, the sound harsh and unnatural. "You don't get it, do you? This isn't just some ghost story. Lady Phillips isn't just haunting this place—she's *judging* it. Judging us."

Bella's face paled. "Judging us? For what?"

"For being exactly what she hated," Jamie said, his tone sharp. "Spoiled. Arrogant. Uncaring. We've all done something to deserve this, whether you want to admit it or not."

"I haven't done anything!" Olivia snapped, her voice rising. "I don't deserve this!"

Jamie turned to her, his gaze cold. "Are you sure about that?"

Olivia faltered, taking another step back. "What's that supposed to mean?"

"It means none of us are innocent," Jamie said. "And she's going to make us pay."

The group stood in stunned silence, the weight of Jamie's words pressing down on them. Finally, Lucy spoke, her voice barely above a whisper. "Jamie... what did she do to you?"

Jamie looked at her, his expression unreadable. "She made me feel what it's like to be powerless. To have no control. To be nothing but a toy in someone else's hands. And when she was done..." He trailed off, his hands clenching into fists.

"When she was done, what?" Bella pressed, though her voice was shaky.

Jamie's lips curled into a bitter smile. "She let me go. For now. But she's not done. Not with me, and definitely not with you."

A loud crash from upstairs made everyone jump. The sound was followed by the unmistakable creak of footsteps descending the staircase—slow, deliberate, and impossibly loud.

"She's coming," Jamie whispered.

The group turned toward the staircase, their fear palpable. The shadows at the top of the stairs seemed to writhe and twist, growing darker with each passing second. Bella clung to Lucy, her breath coming in shallow gasps, while Olivia and Dane stood frozen, unable to tear their eyes away from the looming darkness.

"Jamie," Lucy said, her voice trembling. "We have to get out of here."

"There's no way out," Jamie said flatly. "Not until she's done with us."

"That's insane!" Olivia shouted. "You can't seriously believe that we're trapped here because of some ghost!"

"Believe what you want," Jamie said, his tone cold. "But if you think you can just walk out of here, you're wrong. She won't let you."

Olivia's eyes darted to the door, her mind racing. "I'm not staying here to find out what she wants.

If you want to sit around and wait for her to kill you, fine. But I'm leaving."

Before anyone could stop her, Olivia bolted for the front door. She grabbed the handle and pulled, but the door didn't budge. She yanked harder, her movements growing frantic. "It's locked!" she screamed, pounding on the heavy wood. "Let me out!"

"It's not locked," Jamie said quietly. "She's holding it shut."

"That's ridiculous!" Olivia shouted, her voice rising. "It's just a door!"

"Try breaking it, then," Jamie said with a shrug. "See what happens."

Dane stepped forward, his jaw set. "This is ridiculous. If she won't open it, I will."

He grabbed a nearby chair and swung it at the door with all his strength. The chair shattered on impact, splinters flying everywhere, but the door remained unscathed. Not even a scratch.

Olivia turned back to the group, her face pale and tear-streaked. "What do we do?" she whispered.

Jamie's gaze shifted to the shadows at the top of the staircase, where the footsteps had stopped.

The air grew colder, and the oppressive presence in the room became almost unbearable.

"We wait," Jamie said, his voice barely audible. "And we pray she's merciful."

From the darkness at the top of the stairs, a figure began to emerge—a tall, shadowy silhouette with an aura of cold malice. The group froze, their terror complete as Lady Phillips finally made her presence known

Chapter 11:

No Way Out

The cold presence of Lady Phillips lingered in the air, even as her silhouette disappeared back into the shadows. The group stood frozen, too terrified to speak, their breaths coming in sharp, shallow gasps. Finally, Olivia broke the silence, her voice high-pitched and cracking.

"She's not real. She can't be real," she muttered, pacing back and forth like a trapped animal. "This is all some kind of... some kind of sick joke!"

Bella shook her head, her wide eyes fixed on the staircase. "You saw her. We all did. She's real, Olivia."

"Don't say that!" Olivia snapped, spinning to face her. "Don't you dare say that! This isn't happening. It's not!"

"Enough!" Dane barked, slamming his empty whiskey glass onto the table with a sharp crack. "Panicking isn't going to help us. We need to figure out how to get out of here."

"How, Dane?" Lucy demanded, her voice trembling. "The doors won't open, the windows won't break, and she's... she's everywhere. You saw what happened when Jamie tried to mock her."

"Then we stop mocking her," Dane said, his jaw tight. "We stay calm, stay together, and—"

"Stay together?" Olivia interrupted, her laughter hysterical. "Are you serious? You really think holding hands and singing Kumbaya is going to stop her from killing us? We're trapped! She's going to pick us off one by one, and it's going to be your fault if we sit here and wait for it!"

"*My* fault?" Dane shot back, his face reddening. "I didn't bring us here, Olivia. Jamie did. Why don't you go yell at him?"

"Oh, right, because he's so helpful right now," Olivia snapped, gesturing to where Jamie stood silently, staring into space. "He's already broken."

"Maybe because he's seen what's coming," Lucy said softly, her voice trembling.

As the tension in the group reached a boiling point, Bella stood from her chair, crossing the room to Jamie. Her movements were hesitant, but her voice carried a pleading edge.

"Jamie," she said, touching his arm gently. "You have to help us. You know what she wants. You've seen her. Tell us how to get out of this."

Jamie turned his head slowly, his eyes meeting hers. For a moment, something flickered in his gaze—recognition, regret, something human. But it was fleeting. He shook his head.

"There's no way out," he murmured. "She's not going to stop."

Bella's hand slid from his arm, her face crumpling. "You're just going to give up? That's it?"

"I'm not giving up," Jamie said, his voice hollow. "I'm surviving. She's made her judgment. Now it's just a matter of time."

Across the room, Olivia scoffed. "Oh, that's comforting. Thanks for the pep talk, Jamie."

Dane, clearly frustrated, stood abruptly. "We can't just sit here. There has to be a way out.

Maybe there's a cellar or a servant's passage—something we haven't found yet."

"And what if there's not?" Lucy asked, her voice small.

"Then we keep looking," Dane said, his tone sharp. "Unless you want to sit here and wait to die."

Olivia snorted. "You're just trying to play hero so you can feel like a big man."

"Shut up, Olivia," Dane growled, stepping closer to her. "You're not helping."

"And what are you doing? Huh? Acting tough? Barking orders? You don't have a clue what you're doing, Dane, so stop pretending you're in charge!"

"I'm trying to keep us alive!" Dane snapped, his voice rising. "Which is more than I can say for you, pacing around like a lunatic."

The argument escalated quickly, the fear and stress boiling over into shouting. Bella stepped back toward Jamie, her hands trembling, while Lucy stood frozen in the corner, tears streaming silently down her face.

"You think I'm the problem?" Olivia spat. "You're the one who can't handle the pressure, Dane. You're just a drunk with a superiority complex!"

"Better than a self-absorbed princess who runs at the first sign of trouble!" Dane shot back. "You think you're better than the rest of us? Newsflash: you're just as screwed as we are!"

"Stop it!" Bella shouted, her voice breaking. "This isn't helping! Can't you see? This is what she wants. She's turning us against each other!"

For a moment, the room fell silent, her words sinking in. But the tension didn't ease—it shifted, simmering just beneath the surface.

Dane turned suddenly, heading for the grand window at the far end of the room. "I'm not waiting around for her to come back. If the doors won't open, I'll smash my way out of here."

"You've already tried that!" Olivia snapped. "It doesn't work!"

"Then I'll find another way," Dane said through gritted teeth. He grabbed a heavy candlestick from the mantle and swung it at the glass with all his strength. The window shuddered but didn't break. He swung again, harder this time, and a spiderweb of cracks spread across the pane. "See?" he said triumphantly. "It's breaking. One more—"

Before he could finish, the glass repaired itself before their eyes, the cracks disappearing as though they'd never existed. Dane stumbled back, his face pale. "What the hell?"

"She's not going to let us leave," Jamie said flatly. "You're wasting your energy."

Dane turned on him, his fists clenched. "You knew this would happen, didn't you? That's why you're so calm—you already gave up!"

"Dane, stop!" Bella said, stepping between them. "Fighting won't help."

"He's just sitting there like a coward!" Dane shouted. "While the rest of us—"

The room went dark again, the temperature dropping sharply. A low, guttural laugh echoed through the air, freezing them all in place.

"You cannot run," a cold voice whispered, sending shivers down their spines. "You cannot hide. Judgment is coming."

The lights flickered back on, revealing the group huddled together in terror. On the far wall, the words *ALL WILL PAY* were scrawled in blackened soot, the letters dripping as though freshly burned.

Bella let out a sob, clutching at Lucy. "What do we do?"

Jamie stepped forward, his voice low and steady. "We wait."

"For what?" Olivia asked, her voice trembling.

Jamie's gaze shifted to the staircase, where the shadows were beginning to move again.

"For her."

Chapter 12:

Paranoia in the Shadows

The words *ALL WILL PAY* glistened on the wall as though they were alive, the dark letters pulsing faintly before fading into the woodwork. No one moved, the air in the room thick with dread. It felt as if the Hall itself were holding its breath, waiting for the next moment to strike.

Bella clung to Lucy, her sobs muffled against her friend's shoulder. Olivia paced again, her footsteps frantic and uneven, muttering under her breath about ways to escape. Dane stood by the fireplace, staring at the soot-streaked wall, his jaw tight and his knuckles white as he gripped the shattered remnants of the candlestick. Jamie remained still, his eyes locked on the staircase, his expression blank but tense.

"She's not going to stop," Jamie murmured, breaking the silence. His voice was low and hollow, carrying the weight of something they couldn't yet understand.

"Shut up," Olivia hissed, spinning to face him. "You don't know anything. You don't know what's going to happen."

Jamie's gaze didn't waver. "I know enough."

Dane scoffed, his laugh harsh and bitter. "Great. So we've got the prophet of doom over here, telling us we're all screwed. Real helpful, Jamie."

"I'm just saying the truth," Jamie said calmly, not rising to the bait.

"Yeah? Well, how about you keep it to yourself for a change?" Dane snapped, his frustration bubbling over. "Because sitting here listening to you talk about how hopeless everything is? That's not going to save us."

"Nothing's going to save us," Jamie replied, his tone unnervingly even.

Olivia stopped pacing and jabbed a finger in Jamie's direction. "You're loving this, aren't you?" she spat. "The big, dramatic speech about how we're all doomed, while you just sit there and do nothing."

"I'm not 'loving' anything," Jamie replied, his gaze unwavering. "But fighting each other isn't going to stop her."

"Oh, and what will?" Olivia shot back. "Sitting here like lambs to the slaughter?"

"She's right," Dane said, turning to the group. "We can't just sit here. We have to do something."

"Like what?" Lucy asked, her voice trembling. "We've tried everything. The doors, the windows—she's not letting us leave."

"Then we fight," Dane said, his jaw tightening. "If she wants to come after us, fine. Let her. But I'm not going down without a fight."

"And how, exactly, do you plan to fight a ghost?" Jamie asked, his tone almost amused. "Punch the air? Throw furniture around? Good luck with that."

Dane took a step toward him, his eyes blazing. "You've got a lot to say for someone who's done nothing but sit on his ass and mope since this started."

"Because I know what's coming," Jamie snapped, his voice rising. "And you can't fight her. You can't fight what's already decided."

Before Dane could respond, the sound of slow, deliberate footsteps echoed down the hallway. The group froze, their argument forgotten as they turned toward the open doorway. The footsteps grew louder, closer, but the hallway beyond remained empty.

"Jamie..." Bella whispered, clutching his arm. "What's happening?"

"She's toying with us," Jamie said softly. "Testing us."

Olivia backed away from the door, her hands trembling. "I can't do this. I can't just stand here and wait for her to... to—"

"Shh!" Lucy hissed, grabbing her arm. "Do you hear that?"

The footsteps stopped abruptly, replaced by a faint whispering sound. It was soft at first, barely audible, but it grew steadily louder, a chorus of voices murmuring unintelligibly. The sound seemed to come from everywhere and nowhere, surrounding them.

"What are they saying?" Bella asked, her voice trembling.

"Nothing you want to hear," Jamie replied.

The whispers stopped suddenly, replaced by a deafening bang. The chandelier above them swung wildly, its crystals clinking together in a chaotic symphony. Bella screamed, pulling Lucy down as shards of glass rained down from one of the broken arms.

Dane grabbed Olivia and dragged her toward the wall, shielding her as the chandelier swayed dangerously above them. Jamie stood his ground, his expression unreadable.

The cold voice from before echoed through the room, sending chills down their spines. "The time for judgment is near."

The lights flickered violently, casting the room into alternating moments of blinding brightness and total darkness. In the confusion, Bella stumbled toward the corner, pulling Lucy with her. Olivia screamed as the doors to the dining room slammed shut, trapping them inside.

"What does she want?" Lucy cried, her voice breaking.

"Revenge," Jamie said simply, stepping forward. "She's judging us. All of us."

"For what?" Bella asked, her tears streaming down her face. "We haven't done anything!"

"Are you sure about that?" Jamie asked, his tone sharp. "Think hard, Bella. Everyone here has something they're hiding. Something they're ashamed of."

"Shut up, Jamie!" Olivia shouted, her voice raw. "This isn't the time for your games."

Jamie smirked faintly, though there was no humor in it. "It's not a game. It's the truth. And she already knows it."

The room fell silent again, the air thick with tension. From somewhere above, the sound of a door creaking open echoed through the Hall.

"She's coming," Jamie said softly. "And there's nothing you can do to stop her."

The group huddled together as the oppressive presence in the room grew stronger, the temperature dropping to near-freezing. The shadows on the walls seemed to stretch and twist, forming shapes that didn't belong.

And then, from the darkness at the far end of the room, a figure began to emerge. Tall and imposing, her outline flickered like a candle flame, her eyes glowing with cold malice.

Lady Phillips had arrived.

Chapter 13:

The Secrets Revealed

Lady Phillips stood at the far end of the room, her towering figure cloaked in shadow and malice. Her presence froze the air, and the group huddled closer together, their breaths visible in the cold. Her eyes glowed faintly, their light piercing the darkness, and when she finally spoke, her voice was low and sharp, cutting through the silence like a blade.

"You have all been weighed," she said, her words echoing unnaturally. "And you have been found wanting."

Bella whimpered, clutching Lucy's arm as if the contact could shield her from the cold gaze of Lady Phillips. Dane stepped forward instinctively, his jaw tight, his fists clenched at his sides.

"What do you want from us?" he demanded, his voice shaking despite his bravado. "We didn't do anything to you!"

Lady Phillips turned her glowing eyes to Dane, her lips curling into a cold smile. "Didn't you?" she asked. Her voice seemed to grow louder, surrounding them from all sides. "Shall I remind you of your sins?"

Before Dane could respond, the air around him grew heavier. He staggered back, his hands flying to his head as though trying to block out something only he could hear. His breaths came in short gasps, his defiance crumbling under the weight of Lady Phillips' gaze.

"You pride yourself on being the strong one," she said, her tone mocking. "The protector. But tell me, who protected your friend when you betrayed him?"

Dane's eyes widened, his lips trembling. "I-I don't know what you're talking about," he stammered.

Lady Phillips raised a hand, and the room filled with the sound of laughter—Dane's laughter. The others flinched as the sound grew louder, harsher, until it was almost a roar. Images flickered in the air, like a film projected onto the walls. A younger Dane sat at a poker table, grinning as he raked in a pile of chips. Across from him sat another man, his face pale, his hands shaking as he pushed a document across the table.

"That was his deed," Lady Phillips said coldly. "The deed to his home. You took everything he had, knowing he couldn't win. Knowing he'd lose his family because of you."

"It was just a game!" Dane shouted, his voice breaking. "He knew the risks! It's not my fault he—"

"Lost his home," Lady Phillips finished. "His wife. His life."

The room fell silent as the images disappeared, leaving Dane shaking in the center of the group. Bella's hand flew to her mouth, her eyes wide with horror.

"You drove him to ruin," Lady Phillips said, her voice like ice. "And now you will feel what it is to lose everything."

Dane stumbled back, his face pale. "No... no, please—"

But Lady Phillips' gaze turned elsewhere, as though Dane were no longer worth her time.

"Who's next?" Lady Phillips murmured, her voice sending shivers down their spines. Her glowing eyes settled on Olivia, who flinched as if struck.

"I didn't do anything," Olivia said quickly, her voice high-pitched and frantic. "You've got the wrong person!"

Lady Phillips tilted her head, a cruel smile playing at her lips. "Haven't I? Let us see."

The room darkened, and Olivia let out a strangled cry as a new set of images appeared on the walls. This time, they showed Olivia standing in a lavish boutique, her arms laden with shopping bags. Behind her, a young man stood at the register, his face red as he handed over a black credit card.

"You've built your life on the backs of others," Lady Phillips said. "Taking without giving. Bleeding dry those who trusted you."

"That's not true!" Olivia shouted, shaking her head. "I—I paid him back—"

"Did you?" Lady Phillips interrupted, her voice growing colder. The images shifted, showing the young man sitting in a darkened room, his head in his hands. "He lost everything because of you. His money. His trust. His heart. All so you could live your life of indulgence."

Olivia fell to her knees, tears streaming down her face. "I didn't mean to hurt him," she whispered. "I didn't think—"

"No," Lady Phillips said sharply. "You didn't think. You didn't care. And now, you will feel the weight of what you've done."

The glow in her eyes intensified, and Olivia screamed, clutching at her head as though trying to block out the images. But Lady Phillips had already moved on.

Bella backed away, her heart pounding as Lady Phillips' gaze fell on her. "No," she whispered, shaking her head. "Please, no..."

"You hide behind your innocence," Lady Phillips said, her voice almost soft. "But no one is truly innocent, are they?"

The images this time were softer, almost serene— Bella sitting at a desk, a warm smile on her face as she spoke to an elderly woman across from her. But the elderly woman's expression was uncertain, her hands wringing nervously.

"You were kind," Lady Phillips said, her tone laced with mockery. "So kind, so gentle. She trusted you completely."

The images shifted, showing Bella slipping papers into her bag as the elderly woman signed a document. Bella's face was calm, but her eyes betrayed her—calculating, cold.

"No!" Bella cried, shaking her head. "That's not what happened! I didn't—"

"You took her savings," Lady Phillips said, her voice cutting through Bella's protests. "Her life's work. And when she realized what you had done, you were already gone."

Tears streamed down Bella's face as she collapsed to the floor, her sobs echoing through the room. "I didn't mean to hurt her," she whispered. "I was desperate..."

Lady Phillips turned away, her expression one of icy satisfaction. "Desperation is no excuse for betrayal."

Lucy was the only one left untouched, her face pale and her body trembling as she clutched the back of a chair for support. Lady Phillips turned her glowing gaze to Lucy, her smile growing wider.

"And now," she said softly, "the one who hides the most."

Lucy's breath caught in her throat, her legs threatening to give way beneath her. "No," she whispered. "Please..."

Lady Phillips stepped closer, her presence suffocating. "It is time for your sins to be laid bare."

The room plunged into darkness.

Chapter 14:

Lucy's Sin

The room was deathly silent as the group turned their eyes toward Lucy. She stood trembling, her hands gripping the back of the chair as if it were the only thing keeping her upright. Her chest heaved as she fought to catch her breath, her face pale as Lady Phillips' glowing gaze settled on her.

"No," Lucy whispered, her voice trembling. "Not me. Please, not me."

Lady Phillips tilted her head, her expression a mixture of curiosity and cold malice. "Ah, the quiet one," she said, her voice soft but laced with venom. "Always watching. Always pretending. But the weight of your guilt has never left you, has it?"

"I don't know what you're talking about," Lucy stammered, shaking her head furiously. "I haven't done anything!"

Lady Phillips smiled, a cold, sharp smile that sent shivers racing down their spines. "Haven't you?" She raised a hand, and the shadows on the walls began to move, forming images that danced like firelight.

The others watched in stunned silence as the scene unfolded.

The images showed Lucy sitting in a café, her hair pulled back into a neat bun and her hands wrapped around a steaming cup of coffee. Across from her sat another woman, younger and smiling nervously. She was talking animatedly, her hands gesturing as she spoke, her face glowing with excitement.

"That's my best friend," Lucy said quietly, her voice trembling. "That's... that's Emma."

"Yes," Lady Phillips said, her tone mocking. "Your best friend. The one who trusted you with her dreams, her secrets, her heart."

The images shifted, showing Lucy and Emma walking down a busy street, Emma pointing excitedly at a shop window displaying wedding dresses. Lucy smiled, but there was something in her eyes—something dark, calculating.

"You smiled while she shared her joy," Lady Phillips said. "But what were you thinking, Lucy? What did you hide behind that smile?"

Lucy's breath hitched, and her knees buckled slightly. "I didn't mean to..."

The scene changed again. This time, Lucy stood in a dimly lit room, her phone pressed to her ear. Her voice was soft but sharp, her tone laced with bitterness. "She doesn't deserve him," Lucy said, her lips curling into a sneer. "He's too good for her. She's just... a child playing dress-up. She doesn't even know what she's doing."

The others stared at Lucy in shock as the words filled the room, echoing like a sinister chant. Bella gasped, her hand flying to her mouth. "Lucy..."

"I didn't mean it," Lucy said quickly, tears streaming down her face. "I was jealous. She had everything—a fiancé, a future. I... I just wanted what she had."

Lady Phillips stepped closer, her gaze piercing. "And what did you do, Lucy? How far did your jealousy take you?"

The images shifted one final time, showing Emma standing alone in a crowded room, her face pale and her eyes glistening with tears. She clutched a crumpled letter in her hands, her lips trembling as she tried to hold herself together.

"She found your letter," Lady Phillips said, her voice a whisper that seemed to fill every corner of the room. "The letter you sent to her fiancé. The lies you told about her. The doubts you planted in his mind."

"No!" Lucy cried, collapsing to her knees. "I didn't mean for her to find it! I just wanted... I just wanted him to see the truth."

"The truth?" Lady Phillips' voice turned icy. "Or your version of it? You tore apart her life because you couldn't stand to see her happy. And what was your reward, Lucy? Did her pain bring you joy?"

Lucy sobbed, shaking her head violently. "No... I just... I just wanted her to hurt like I did."

"And hurt she did," Lady Phillips said coldly. "Her engagement ended. Her dreams shattered. And she never spoke to you again."

The images faded, leaving Lucy kneeling on the floor, her body trembling as her sobs filled the silence. The others stared at her, their expressions ranging from shock to disgust.

Lady Phillips stepped closer, towering over Lucy like a dark specter. "You hid behind your silence, behind your smiles, but your sins have always been with you. You will feel the weight of what you've done, just as she did."

Lucy looked up at her, her tear-streaked face pale. "Please," she whispered. "I'll make it right. I'll... I'll apologize. I'll—"

"There is no apology for a broken heart," Lady Phillips said sharply. "No way to undo the damage you caused. You have been judged."

The air around Lucy grew colder, and the others stepped back instinctively as a shadow fell over her. Lucy cried out, clutching at her chest as though an invisible hand were pressing down on her. Her sobs turned to gasps, and then silence.

When the shadow lifted, Lucy lay slumped on the floor, her eyes closed, her face frozen in an expression of despair.

Bella let out a strangled cry, covering her face with her hands. "She's gone," she whispered. "She's really gone."

Lady Phillips turned her gaze to the remaining three, her smile growing wider. "And now," she said softly, "who will be next?"

The room fell into silence once more, broken only by the faint sound of footsteps echoing from somewhere deep within the Hall. Jamie, Bella, and Olivia exchanged terrified glances, each of them silently pleading not to be the next to face Lady Phillips' judgment.

The air grew colder again, and Lady Phillips raised her hand, pointing directly at Bella.

"You."

Chapter 15:

The Aftermath

The silence in the room was suffocating, broken only by Bella's soft, uneven breaths and the faint crackling of the dying fire in the hearth. Lucy's lifeless body lay crumpled on the floor, her tear streaked face frozen in despair. No one dared move. Even Lady Phillips, her towering form still and menacing, seemed to relish the quiet horror her actions had left behind.

Bella was the first to speak, her voice barely above a whisper. "She's... dead," she said, her words trembling as her gaze darted between Lucy and Lady Phillips. "You killed her."

Lady Phillips didn't respond. She simply stood there, her glowing eyes cold and unfeeling.

Olivia stepped back, her hands trembling. "No," she muttered, her voice shaky and frantic. "This isn't happening. It's not real. She can't be dead. She's just... unconscious. That's all."

Jamie leaned against the wall, his face pale but otherwise unreadable. "She's not unconscious," he said flatly. "She's gone. And if we don't figure this out, we'll be next."

"Shut up!" Olivia shouted, spinning to face him. Her face was flushed with panic, her hands balled into fists. "You don't know that! We can still get out of here. We just have to—"

"There is no getting out," Jamie interrupted, his voice harsh. "I've been trying to tell you that from the beginning. The Hall has us. She has us. The sooner you accept that, the better."

"You're just giving up?" Bella asked, her voice rising as tears streamed down her face. "That's your plan? To stand there and wait for her to kill us?"

"What other choice do we have?" Jamie snapped. "You saw what happened to Lucy. She didn't even fight back. She just... let it happen."

"That's not true," Bella said, shaking her head. "Lucy didn't deserve this. None of us do."

Lady Phillips finally spoke, her voice sharp and cutting. "You still cling to your innocence," she said, her gaze fixed on Bella. "But it will not save you."

Bella flinched, taking a step back. "I didn't do anything," she said quickly, her voice trembling. "I swear, I didn't."

"You'll say anything to save yourself, won't you?" Olivia said bitterly. "You're no better than the rest of us, Bella. None of us are."

"Stop it!" Bella shouted, her voice breaking. "This isn't helping. Fighting with each other isn't going to stop her."

"It doesn't matter what we do," Jamie said, his tone grim. "She's already made up her mind."

Olivia turned on Jamie, her panic morphing into anger. "You don't know that! You think you're so smart, so above everything, but you're just as scared as the rest of us. You're just too much of a coward to admit it."

Jamie's jaw tightened, but he didn't respond. His silence only fueled Olivia's rage.

"You're the reason we're here," she continued, her voice rising. "You brought us to this godforsaken house, and now we're all going to die because of you!"

"I didn't force you to come," Jamie shot back, his voice cold. "You could've said no."

"Oh, don't give me that," Olivia spat. "You knew exactly what you were doing. You wanted to show off, to rub your money and your stupid inheritance in our faces. And now look where we are!"

Bella stepped between them, holding up her hands. "Stop it! Both of you. This isn't helping."

"She's right," Jamie said, his voice softer now but no less firm. "You can yell at me all you want, but it won't change anything. The Hall doesn't care about your tantrums. She doesn't care."

Bella turned to Lady Phillips, her tear-streaked face desperate. "Please," she said, her voice shaking. "You've made your point. We understand. We're sorry. Just... let us go."

Lady Phillips tilted her head, her glowing eyes narrowing. "Sorry?" she said, her tone laced with disdain. "Do you think your apologies will undo the pain you've caused? The lives you've ruined?"

Bella sobbed, her knees threatening to give way. "I'll make it right," she whispered. "I swear, I'll make it right."

"You cannot undo what has been done," Lady Phillips said sharply. "But you will feel the weight of your sins."

Bella let out a strangled cry, her hands covering her face. Olivia backed away from the group, her movements frantic and erratic.

"There has to be a way out," Olivia muttered to herself, her eyes darting around the room. "There has to be. There's always a way."

"There isn't," Jamie said, his voice flat.

"There has to be!" Olivia screamed, spinning to face him. "I'm not going to die here! Do you hear me? I'm not going to die here!"

Lady Phillips smiled faintly, her gaze shifting to Bella once more. "You may run," she said softly. "But you cannot hide."

Bella's sobs grew louder as Olivia backed further toward the shadows, her movements jerky and panicked. Jamie remained still, his expression grim, as Lady Phillips stepped closer to Bella.

The glow in her eyes intensified, casting long shadows across the room. "Now," she said, her voice cold and commanding. "It is your turn."

Bella looked up at her, her face streaked with tears, and let out a trembling whisper. "Please... don't."

The room fell silent, the air heavy with anticipation. And then, the shadows surged forward.

Chapter 16

Bella's Judgment

Bella trembled as the shadows crept closer, coiling around her feet like snakes. The oppressive cold wrapped itself around her, and the air seemed to press against her chest, making it hard to breathe. She clutched the back of a chair for support, her knees threatening to buckle.

"Please," Bella whispered, her voice trembling. "Please, I'll do anything. Don't hurt me."

Lady Phillips moved closer, her towering form casting a long shadow across the room. Her glowing eyes bore into Bella's, and her lips curled into a cruel smile. "Anything?" she repeated mockingly. "Anything to save yourself. Just like always."

The room darkened again, and the flickering candlelight was replaced by moving images on the walls—Bella's past playing out like a twisted film reel for everyone to see.

The first image showed Bella in a sleek office, sitting across from an elderly woman. The woman looked frail, her hands shaking as she handed Bella a document. Bella's professional smile didn't falter, but her eyes gleamed with calculation.

"You preyed on the weak," Lady Phillips said, her voice cold. "You built a life of comfort by taking from those who had little."

Bella shook her head, tears streaming down her face. "No! That's not true. I was helping them."

"Helping?" Lady Phillips snapped. The image changed, showing Bella sliding the document into her bag as the elderly woman looked away. "You told her she was investing in her future. That her savings would grow. But you knew better, didn't you?"

The scene shifted again. The same elderly woman now sat in a tiny apartment, her hands clutching a letter. Tears streamed down her face as she read the words, her body wracked with silent sobs.

"She lost everything," Lady Phillips said, her tone dripping with disdain. "Her home. Her security. Her dignity. And what did you do, Bella? Did you look back? Did you care?"

"No," Bella whispered, shaking her head. "I didn't know... I didn't think it would..."

"You didn't care," Lady Phillips finished coldly. "You took her trust and turned it into profit. And when her life fell apart, you moved on without a second thought."

The others watched in stunned silence, the weight of Bella's actions settling over them like a storm cloud. Olivia's mouth opened and closed, but no words came. Jamie stared at Bella, his face unreadable.

"You lied to us," Olivia finally said, her voice laced with disgust. "You pretended to be so sweet, so innocent, and all this time you were just... just a thief."

"I didn't mean to hurt anyone!" Bella sobbed, falling to her knees. "I just... I needed the money. I didn't think..."

"You didn't think," Lady Phillips echoed, her voice sharp. "And now you will understand what it feels like to be helpless. To be powerless."

The shadows around Bella thickened, rising like a tide. She let out a strangled cry, her hands clutching at the floor as if she could anchor herself. The cold grew more intense, and the air seemed to hum with unseen energy.

"Please!" Bella begged, her voice breaking. "I'll give it back! I'll make it right!"

"There is no going back," Lady Phillips said, her voice as unyielding as stone. "You took her future. Now I will take yours."

The shadows surged forward, engulfing Bella completely. Her screams echoed through the room, filled with terror and despair, before cutting off abruptly. When the darkness receded, Bella was gone.

All that remained was the faint outline of her body scorched into the wooden floor, a blackened shadow burned into the grain.

The remaining two—Jamie and Olivia—stood frozen, their faces pale and their bodies trembling. Lady Phillips turned to them slowly, her glowing eyes narrowing.

"Two remain," she said softly, her smile growing wider. "Shall we see who is next?"

Her gaze shifted to Olivia, who stumbled back, shaking her head violently. "No," she whispered. "No, no, no..."

But the shadows were already moving.

Chapter 17:

Olivia's Desperate Escape

"No," Olivia whispered, shaking her head furiously as the shadows began creeping toward her. "No, this isn't happening. I'm not staying here. I'm not going to die like this!"

She backed away, her chest heaving as her panic took over. Her eyes darted between Jamie, Lady Phillips, and the door, calculating her odds. She had to get out. Somehow, she had to get out.

"Olivia," Jamie said flatly, his voice low and grim. "You can't escape. The Hall won't let you."

"Shut up!" she screamed, her voice cracking. "You don't know that! You don't know anything!"

Lady Phillips tilted her head, watching Olivia with a cold, detached amusement. "Run, little mouse," she said softly. "It will not matter."

Olivia let out a strangled cry and bolted for the door. Her heels clacked against the wooden floor as she threw herself at the heavy oak door and wrenched at the handle. It didn't budge.

"Open!" she shouted, her voice raw with desperation. "OPEN!"

She slammed her fists against the door, kicking and clawing at it like a caged animal. The shadows crept closer, curling around her feet like tendrils of smoke. She screamed, her terror giving her a burst of strength as she threw her entire body against the door. It shuddered but didn't give way.

"Let me out!" she sobbed, pounding against the unyielding wood. "Please, let me out!"

The temperature in the room dropped sharply, and Olivia let out a yelp as frost began to spread across the edges of the door, freezing her hands where they gripped the handle. She stumbled back, cradling her hands against her chest, her breath coming in ragged gasps.

Behind her, Lady Phillips watched silently, her glowing eyes fixed on Olivia like a predator toying with its prey. Jamie remained still, his face pale, his arms crossed tightly over his chest as if bracing himself for what was to come.

"You can't escape her," Jamie said softly. "She'll find you no matter where you go."

Olivia spun around, her face contorted with rage and fear. "You don't get to talk to me like that! You don't get to act like you're above all this! You brought us here, Jamie. This is your fault!"

Jamie didn't respond, his expression unchanged. His silence only seemed to fuel Olivia's anger.

"You're a coward," she spat. "You think if you just stand there and take it, you'll survive? You won't. None of us will."

"I know," Jamie said simply.

Olivia turned back to the door, her mind racing. She couldn't stay here. She couldn't let Lady Phillips judge her. She had to find another way out. Her eyes scanned the room, landing on the large bay window near the fireplace.

She rushed toward it, grabbing a heavy iron candlestick from the mantle. The frost on the glass sparkled in the dim light, taunting her with its beauty. "If the door won't open, the window will," she muttered to herself, as if saying it out loud would make it true.

"Olivia, don't," Jamie said, his tone sharp. "The Hall won't let you."

"Shut up!" she screamed, swinging the candlestick with all her might. The window cracked, a spiderweb of fractures spreading across the glass. She swung again, harder this time, and a piece of glass fell away, leaving a jagged opening.

She dropped the candlestick and reached through the broken pane, ignoring the shards that sliced into her skin. The cold night air hit her face, sharp and biting, but it was a relief—a sign that freedom was just within reach.

"I'm getting out of here," she muttered, pulling herself up onto the window ledge. She glanced back at Jamie, her bloodied hands gripping the frame. "You can stay here and die if you want, but I'm not going to let her take me."

As Olivia hoisted herself through the window, she felt a strange resistance, as if the air itself were pressing against her. Her breath quickened, her heart pounding as she pushed harder, her body halfway out the window.

The shadows surged forward suddenly, wrapping around her legs like iron chains. She screamed, clawing at the frame as they began to pull her back inside.

"No!" she shrieked, her voice breaking. "No, no, no! Let me go!"

The frost on the window spread rapidly, encasing her arms and shoulders, trapping her in place. The shadows twisted around her, pulling harder, and her screams turned to sobs as her strength began to fade.

"You cannot run from judgment," Lady Phillips said, her voice echoing through the room. "You cannot escape what you have earned."

Olivia let out one last, desperate cry as the shadows yanked her back inside. Her body hit the floor with a sickening thud, and the frost melted away, leaving her shivering and gasping for air.

Jamie stared at Olivia as she lay on the floor, her body trembling and her eyes wide with terror. She clutched her chest, her breaths ragged, and whispered, "She won't let us go... She won't let any of us go..."

Lady Phillips stepped closer, her smile growing wider. "Correct," she said softly. Her glowing eyes shifted to Jamie. "And now, the one who led them here."

The air in the room grew heavier, and Jamie straightened, his jaw tightening as he braced himself for what was to come.

Chapter 18:

Olivia's Breaking Point

Olivia lay crumpled on the cold wooden floor, her body trembling as she struggled to catch her breath. Her bloodied hands clutched at her chest, her fingers curling into the fabric of her dress as if to keep herself from unraveling completely. Tears streamed down her face, and her lips moved silently, as though she were trying to say something but no words would come.

Jamie watched her from across the room, his face grim. He didn't move, didn't speak, just stood there with his arms crossed tightly over his chest. Lady Phillips, towering and menacing, remained still as well, her glowing eyes fixed on Olivia like a predator studying its prey.

"You should have listened," Jamie said finally, his voice low and flat. "I told you there was no way out."

Olivia's head snapped up, her tear-streaked face contorted with rage. "Shut up," she hissed, her voice shaking. "Shut up, Jamie! You don't know anything. You don't know what I've been through."

Jamie's jaw tightened, but he didn't respond.

"You think you're so calm, so smart," Olivia spat, dragging herself into a sitting position. "But you're just as scared as the rest of us. You're just too much of a coward to admit it."

"Coward?" Jamie echoed, his tone sharp. "You're the one who tried to run while the rest of us were still standing here."

Olivia's eyes blazed with fury. "And what was I supposed to do? Just stand here and wait for her to kill me? Like Bella? Like Lucy?"

"She didn't kill them," Jamie said coldly. "She judged them. There's a difference."

Olivia let out a bitter laugh, the sound hollow and broken. "Judged them? Is that what you're calling it? You think this is some kind of trial? It's a massacre, Jamie! We're being hunted."

"No," Lady Phillips interjected, her voice cutting through the argument like a blade. "You are being held accountable."

Olivia turned to Lady Phillips, her chest heaving. "Accountable for what?" she shouted, her voice breaking. "For trying to survive? For doing what I had to do?"

"You did more than survive," Lady Phillips said, her tone laced with disdain. "You thrived at the expense of others. You took without thought, without care, leaving destruction in your wake."

"That's not true!" Olivia screamed, clutching her head. "I didn't destroy anything. I didn't hurt anyone!"

Lady Phillips raised an eyebrow, her smile cold. "Shall we revisit your past? Shall we see the lives you've ruined?"

"No!" Olivia shouted, stumbling to her feet. "No more! I don't want to see it!"

Her eyes darted around the room, looking for anything she could use—any weapon, any escape. But there was nothing. The windows were dark and unyielding, the door firmly shut. The shadows on the walls seemed to pulse with a life of their own, watching, waiting.

Jamie's voice cut through her frantic thoughts. "You can't run from her, Olivia. None of us can."

"I'm not running!" Olivia snapped, though her trembling hands and wild eyes betrayed her. "I'm fighting."

"Fighting who?" Jamie asked, his tone calm but cutting. "Her? Yourself? The truth?"

"Shut up!" Olivia screamed, her voice cracking. She turned to Lady Phillips, her fists clenched. "You don't get to do this. You don't get to judge me. You're just... you're just a ghost!"

Lady Phillips smiled faintly, her glowing eyes narrowing. "A ghost, yes. But one with purpose."

Olivia backed away again, her breathing shallow as she tried to process her situation. She clutched at her hair, her fingers trembling as she tugged at the strands. "This isn't happening," she muttered under her breath. "It's not real. It can't be real."

Jamie's voice came again, low and unrelenting. "It's real, Olivia. And you're next."

"Shut up!" she screamed, her voice raw. She turned to him, her eyes wide with desperation. "Why aren't you doing anything? Why are you just standing there?"

"Because there's nothing to do," Jamie replied, his tone devoid of emotion. "It's already decided."

Olivia let out a choked sob, her hands flying to her face. "No... no, it can't be. I didn't... I didn't deserve this."

Lady Phillips stepped closer, her presence filling the room. "Perhaps you did not think so," she said softly. "But the truth always comes to light."

Olivia backed into the corner, her body pressed against the cold, unyielding wall. Her eyes darted around the room, searching for an escape that wasn't there. Lady Phillips loomed over her, her glowing eyes filled with quiet menace.

"Your time is coming, Olivia," she said, her voice low and commanding. "And there will be no mercy."

Olivia let out a strangled sob as the shadows began to rise once more, swirling around her feet like ink spreading across water. Jamie watched silently, his expression unreadable, as Olivia's screams filled the room.

The lights flickered violently, and then everything went dark.

Chapter 19:

Jamie's Tension

The darkness lingered for what felt like an eternity, broken only by Olivia's strangled sobs and the faint sound of her breathing. Then, with a flicker, the room was bathed in dim, flickering light once more. Olivia sat slumped against the wall, her arms wrapped tightly around her knees. Her face was pale, her lips trembling as she muttered incoherently under her breath. The once fiery, defiant Olivia had crumbled into a shell of herself.

But Jamie barely noticed her. His focus was elsewhere—on Lady Phillips.

The towering specter stood unmoving, her glowing eyes watching Olivia with cold amusement. She had yet to deliver Olivia's full judgment, and Jamie could feel it coming. The tension was suffocating, the air thick with the promise of something terrible. He tried to breathe deeply, but his chest felt tight, as though the Hall itself were pressing down on him.

Jamie's hands clenched into fists at his sides, his nails digging into his palms. He didn't want to admit it, but fear was clawing at him, inching its way into his thoughts. Watching Lucy fall, then Bella, and now Olivia's unraveling—it was like staring into his own future. He knew Lady Phillips would come for him next. She'd said as much.

But he wasn't ready. He wasn't sure he'd ever be ready.

"Jamie," Olivia whispered suddenly, her voice hoarse. She turned her tear-streaked face toward him, her eyes pleading. "Do something."

Jamie didn't respond. He couldn't. What could he do? He'd already tried reasoning with Lady Phillips, tried to ignore her, tried to warn the others—and it had all been useless. The Hall was alive, and Lady Phillips was its judge, jury, and executioner.

"She won't stop," Olivia whispered again, her voice trembling. "She's going to kill us, Jamie. All of us."

Jamie's jaw tightened. "She's not killing us," he said quietly. "She's... holding us accountable." Olivia let out a bitter laugh, the sound hollow and broken. "Is that supposed to make me feel better?"

"It's the truth," Jamie said, though his voice lacked conviction. "We all did something. That's why she's here."

"And you think you're any better than the rest of us?" Olivia snapped, her voice rising. "You think you don't deserve this? You brought us here, Jamie. This is your fault."

Jamie flinched at her words, though he tried to hide it. "I didn't make you come," he said, his tone defensive. "You chose to be here."

"You knew what this place was!" Olivia shouted, her voice cracking. "You knew about the stories, the ghost—Lady Phillips! And you brought us here anyway, just to show off. Just to feed your ego!"

Jamie opened his mouth to respond, but the words caught in his throat. Was she right? Had he known, deep down, that bringing them to Windermere Hall would end like this? He had brushed off the stories, dismissed the warnings, laughed at the idea of a ghost haunting his family's ancestral home. But now...

Now he wasn't so sure.

Jamie turned away from Olivia, his hands pressed to his temples as he tried to block out her accusations. His mind raced, replaying every decision, every smug comment, every moment of arrogance that had led them to this point. He had always lived for himself—parties, women, money. He'd burned through trust funds and inheritance like they were nothing, leaving a trail of disappointment and destruction in his wake.

And now, Lady Phillips was here to make him pay for it.

He looked up at her, his expression hardening. "So this is it?" he asked, his voice steady despite the tremor in his hands. "This is what you do? You judge people for their mistakes and make them suffer?"

Lady Phillips turned her glowing eyes to him, a faint smile playing at her lips. "Your suffering is not my doing," she said softly. "It is your own."

Jamie took a step forward, his fear giving way to anger. "That's a cop-out. You think you're some righteous avenger, but all you're doing is playing God. Who gave you the right to decide who's guilty and who isn't?"

"Your actions gave me that right," Lady Phillips replied, her voice calm but unyielding. "Your choices. Your arrogance. Your disregard for others."

Jamie's fists clenched again, his anger bubbling over. "You're no better than the rest of us. You're just hiding behind this house, this... this game of judgment. You're nothing but a ghost with a grudge."

Lady Phillips tilted her head, her smile widening. "Perhaps," she said. "But even a ghost with a grudge can bring the truth to light."

The room grew colder, and the shadows on the walls began to move again, twisting and curling like smoke. Jamie felt the weight of the Hall pressing down on him, and for the first time, he couldn't hide the fear in his eyes.

Lady Phillips stepped closer, her glowing eyes locking onto his. "Your time is coming, Jamie Phillips," she said softly. "And when it does, there will be no escape."

Jamie stood his ground, but his heart was pounding. He could feel the walls closing in, the shadows reaching for him. He glanced at Olivia, who was curled in the corner, her wide eyes fixed on him.

And then, as the shadows surged forward, the lights flickered—and went out.

Chapter 20:

Jamie's Judgment

The room was pitch black, the silence heavy and oppressive. Jamie could hear his own breathing—shallow and uneven—as he stood frozen in place. He could feel the weight of Lady Phillips' gaze on him, her cold presence pressing against his chest like an iron hand. He wanted to move, to speak, to fight, but he was paralyzed.

And then, the light returned.

It wasn't the flickering glow of the chandelier or the faint light from the candles. It was a cold, unnatural light, emanating from Lady Phillips herself. She stood before Jamie, her glowing eyes locked onto his, her expression calm and unyielding.

"It is time," she said softly.

Jamie swallowed hard, his hands clenching into fists at his sides. "You've been waiting for this, haven't you?" he said, his voice tight. "You've judged everyone else, and now it's my turn. Fine. Let's get it over with."

Lady Phillips tilted her head slightly, her faint smile laced with something cruel. "So eager to face the truth," she murmured. "But I wonder... will you be so eager when you see it for yourself?"

The shadows on the walls came alive again, twisting and writhing like living creatures. Images flickered in the darkness, each one sharper than the last, each one pulling Jamie deeper into his past. He watched, helpless, as his life played out before him.

The first image was of him as a child, standing in the grand hall of Windermere, his small hands clutching a wooden toy. His parents stood behind him, their faces stern as they scolded him for breaking a priceless vase. The boy in the image didn't cry or apologize. He simply stared back at them, defiant.

"You learned early that consequences could be ignored," Lady Phillips said. "You learned to use your name, your money, your charm to escape the cost of your actions."

The scene shifted. Jamie, now a teenager, leaned against a sleek sports car, laughing with his friends. A man in a shabby suit approached, his face pale as he held out a piece of paper—a notice of repossession. Jamie waved him off with a smirk, tossing a wad of cash at him as if the man were nothing more than a nuisance.

"You turned people into tools," Lady Phillips said, her voice sharp. "Their struggles meant nothing to you. Their pain, invisible."

The images came faster now. Jamie at a party, surrounded by women, his grin wide as he poured expensive champagne into crystal glasses. Jamie at a poker table, laughing as his opponent—an older man with tired eyes—pushed all his chips forward. Jamie standing over a contractor, his arms crossed as he demanded the impossible, ignoring the man's pleas for more time.

"You used people," Lady Phillips said. "Discarded them when they were no longer useful. You built your life on arrogance and greed, believing yourself untouchable."

Jamie stumbled back as the images continued to flood the room, each one a stab to his chest. "Stop it," he muttered, his voice trembling. "That's not who I am. I didn't—"

"You didn't *what*?" Lady Phillips interrupted, her voice rising. "Didn't know? Didn't care? Tell me, Jamie Phillips—what excuse will you use this time?"

"I didn't mean to hurt anyone," Jamie said, his voice breaking. "I was just... I was just living my life."

"Living your life," Lady Phillips repeated coldly. "And what of the lives you destroyed in the process? Were they not worth as much as yours?"

Jamie shook his head, tears streaming down his face. "I didn't know... I didn't think..."

"No," Lady Phillips said sharply. "You did not think. And now, you will feel the weight of every life you've touched. Every person you've broken. Every heart you've shattered."

The shadows surged forward, wrapping around Jamie like chains. He struggled against them, his breaths coming in gasps as they tightened around his chest, his arms, his legs.

"Please," he whispered, his voice barely audible. "Please, I'll change. I'll make it right."

"It is too late," Lady Phillips said, her voice icy. "You have been judged."

The shadows lifted Jamie off the ground, suspending him in the air as the cold grew more intense. His screams filled the room, raw and desperate, as the weight of his guilt crushed him from within. The images on the walls grew brighter, faster, blurring into a whirlwind of pain and regret.

And then, with a deafening crack, it all stopped.

Jamie fell to the floor, his body limp and lifeless. The shadows receded, leaving him lying in a heap at Lady Phillips' feet. His eyes were open, staring blankly at the ceiling, his expression frozen in terror.

Lady Phillips turned away from him, her gaze shifting to Olivia, who sat trembling in the corner. "And so," she said softly, "the last one remains."

Olivia let out a strangled sob, her hands covering her face as Lady Phillips began to move toward her. The air grew colder, the shadows creeping closer, and Olivia's voice broke as she whispered, "Please... please don't..."

Lady Phillips smiled faintly, her glowing eyes narrowing. "There is no escape."

The room fell into darkness once more.

Chapter 21: **The Last One Standing**

The darkness enveloped the room like a shroud, thick and impenetrable. The only sound was Olivia's ragged breathing as she cowered in the corner, her body pressed tightly against the cold stone wall. She could feel the weight of Lady Phillips' gaze even though she couldn't see her. The Hall seemed alive, its very walls humming with anticipation as though it, too, were waiting for the final act to play out.

Jamie's lifeless body lay motionless on the floor, his face frozen in an expression of terror. Olivia couldn't bear to look at him. She couldn't bear to look at anything. All she could do was close her eyes and whisper to herself, hoping against hope that this was all a nightmare she would wake up from.

"It's not real," she muttered under her breath, her voice trembling. "It's not real. It's not real."

But deep down, she knew it was. The icy chill in the air, the oppressive weight pressing down on her chest, the shadows creeping closer with every passing second—it was all too vivid, too visceral to be a dream. This was real. And she was next.

Suddenly, the faintest flicker of light returned to the room, just enough for Olivia to see the dim outline of Lady Phillips standing motionless in the center of the room. Her glowing eyes cut through the darkness, pinning Olivia in place like a predator stalking its prey.

"You cannot hide," Lady Phillips said softly, her voice calm and measured. "There is no escape from the truth."

Olivia's chest tightened, her breaths coming in short, shallow gasps. She pressed herself harder against the wall, her fingers clawing at the stone as if she could somehow dig her way out.

"No," she whispered, her voice barely audible. "I won't let you."

Lady Phillips tilted her head, a faint smile playing at her lips. "Won't you?"

Summoning every ounce of strength she had left, Olivia pushed herself to her feet. Her legs were trembling, her entire body shaking, but she refused to collapse again. She glared at Lady Phillips, her wide eyes brimming with fear and fury.

"I'm not like them," Olivia said, her voice shaking but defiant. "You don't know me. You don't know my life."

Lady Phillips remained silent, her expression unchanged.

"I've made mistakes, sure," Olivia continued, her voice growing louder. "But I don't deserve this. I'm not... I'm not evil. I didn't destroy anyone's life."

"Didn't you?" Lady Phillips asked, her tone soft but sharp as a blade.

Olivia flinched but pressed on. "I did what I had to do. To survive. To succeed. That's what the world is, isn't it? Survival of the fittest."

"The fittest," Lady Phillips echoed, her voice dripping with disdain. "You twist your selfishness into ambition. You call your greed success. But deep down, you know the truth."

Olivia shook her head violently, her hands clenching into fists. "No. You're wrong. I'm not like the others. I don't belong here."

"You brought yourself here," Lady Phillips said simply. "You came willingly. And now you will face the consequences of your choices."

The shadows around Olivia began to shift, growing darker, heavier, more tangible. They seemed to move with purpose, coiling around her feet and slowly climbing her legs like chains. She tried to kick them away, but they held firm, pulling her closer to the center of the room.

"Let me go!" Olivia screamed, her voice cracking. "You can't do this to me!"

Lady Phillips stepped closer, her glowing eyes narrowing. "You cannot run from yourself, Olivia. The shadows are yours. They are your past, your choices, your sins. They are you."

"No!" Olivia shouted, clawing at the tendrils of darkness as they climbed higher, wrapping around her waist. "This isn't fair! You don't get to decide what I deserve!"

Lady Phillips raised a single hand, and the shadows tightened their grip, pulling Olivia to her knees. "Your actions have decided that for you," she said coldly. "I am merely the one who holds the mirror."

Tears streamed down Olivia's face as the weight of Lady Phillips' words pressed against her chest.

She wanted to scream, to fight, to run, but the shadows held her firmly in place. She was trapped, both physically and mentally, unable to escape the inevitability of what was coming.

Jamie's body lay motionless a few feet away, a stark reminder of what awaited her. Lucy and Bella were gone, their fates sealed. She was the last one left, the final piece of Lady Phillips' twisted puzzle.

But something in her refused to give up. Something deep inside her, buried beneath the fear and the guilt, sparked to life.

"You want me to break," Olivia said, her voice trembling but steady. "You want me to fall apart, to admit I'm some horrible person. But I'm not. I'm not perfect, but I'm not a monster. And you... you're just a bully."

Lady Phillips' faint smile faded, replaced by a cold, unreadable expression. "A bully?" she repeated softly.

"That's right," Olivia said, her voice gaining strength. "You hide behind your judgment, pretending you're so righteous, but you're no better than the rest of us. You're just another ghost with a grudge."

The room fell silent, the air thick with tension. For a moment, it seemed as though Lady Phillips might actually respond, might actually acknowledge Olivia's defiance. But then the shadows surged forward again, cutting her off.

Olivia let out a strangled cry as the shadows enveloped her completely, pulling her to the center of the room. Lady Phillips stood over her, her glowing eyes unblinking, her presence cold and unyielding.

"You have spoken your truth," she said softly. "Now you will see mine."

The lights flickered once more, and the room plunged into darkness.

Chapter 22:

Olivia's Judgment

The darkness hung thick and suffocating, broken only by the faint sound of Olivia's ragged breathing. The shadows coiled tighter around her, their grip cold and unyielding. She struggled against them, her arms flailing in vain, but the more she fought, the heavier they became, pulling her closer to the center of the room.

Lady Phillips stood above her, her glowing eyes like beacons in the blackness. Her voice, calm and sharp, pierced the air. "You have run. You have resisted. But you cannot escape the truth, Olivia. It is time to face yourself."

"No!" Olivia screamed, tears streaming down her face. "I don't deserve this! I'm not like them!"

Lady Phillips raised a hand, and the room shifted. The walls became screens, flickering to life with images from Olivia's past. The shadows loosened their grip just enough for Olivia to look up, her wide, terrified eyes locking onto the moving pictures.

The first image showed Olivia sitting in an office, her posture confident, her manicured nails tapping against a polished desk. Across from her sat a younger woman, timid and nervous, holding a portfolio in her trembling hands.

"Do you remember her?" Lady Phillips asked, her voice laced with disdain. "Her name was Rachel. She was fresh out of university, eager to begin her career."

"I... I gave her a chance," Olivia stammered. "I hired her."

"Yes," Lady Phillips said, her tone icy. "You hired her. And then you took her ideas. Her creativity. Her hard work. And you claimed them as your own."

The image shifted, showing Olivia standing in a boardroom, holding up a sleek presentation. The room was filled with applause as her colleagues congratulated her on a "brilliant" proposal. In the background, Rachel sat at her desk, her face pale as she stared at her empty portfolio.

"She trusted you," Lady Phillips continued. "She believed in you. And you stole from her."

"I... I didn't mean to," Olivia whispered, shaking her head. "It wasn't personal. It was just business."

"Just business," Lady Phillips repeated mockingly. "And when she confronted you? When she begged you to give her credit for her work? What did you do?"

The images flickered again, showing Olivia standing over Rachel's desk, her face twisted in anger. "If you can't handle the competition, you don't belong here," Olivia snarled. "Maybe you should find a job more suited to your... talents."

The scene faded, leaving Olivia trembling on the floor. "I didn't know she'd quit," she sobbed. "I didn't know she'd—"

"Lose everything," Lady Phillips finished coldly. "Her career. Her confidence. Her hope."

The images shifted once more, this time showing Olivia at a dinner party. She was laughing, her wine glass held high as she leaned closer to a man seated beside her. His face was familiar— Greg, her best friend's fiancé.

"You played the part well," Lady Phillips said. "The charming friend, the confidant. But what were you whispering in his ear, Olivia?"

Olivia's face twisted in pain as the images played out. She watched herself, lips moving as she planted doubts in Greg's mind. "I just think you deserve better," she whispered. "Someone who really understands you. Someone who won't hold you back."

The images shifted again, showing Greg arguing with Olivia's best friend, their voices raised as Olivia stood nearby, feigning innocence. Then came the final blow: Greg walking out the door, leaving behind the shattered remains of their engagement.

"You destroyed their lives for your own amusement," Lady Phillips said. "You called it harmless fun. But was it harmless for them?"

Olivia sobbed, clutching at her chest. "I didn't mean to hurt her. I didn't mean for it to go that far."

"You never do," Lady Phillips said. "But your actions speak louder than your intentions."

The images began to move faster, flashing through every lie Olivia had told, every person she had betrayed, every life she had manipulated for her own gain. The walls seemed to close in, the weight of her guilt pressing down on her until she could barely breathe.

"Stop," she whispered, her voice hoarse. "Please, stop."

Lady Phillips stepped closer, her glowing eyes narrowing. "Do you see now, Olivia? Do you see the truth?"

Olivia shook her head violently, her tears falling freely. "I'm sorry," she choked out. "I'm so sorry. I'll make it right. I'll fix it."

"There is no fixing the past," Lady Phillips said, her voice cold and final. "There is only judgment."

The shadows surged forward, engulfing Olivia completely. Her screams filled the room, raw and desperate, before being abruptly silenced. When the darkness receded, Olivia was gone.

All that remained was the faint scent of perfume and a single, crumpled photograph of her with Rachel and Greg—her former best friend— smiling together on a sunny day.

Lady Phillips turned slowly, her gaze falling on the now-empty room. The Hall was silent once more, its shadows still and unthreatening. She stepped toward the center of the room, her glowing eyes flickering as they surveyed the aftermath of her work.

"It is done," she murmured.

But deep within the Hall, the faint sound of footsteps echoed—slow, deliberate, and growing louder.

Had the Hall truly finished its reckoning, or was there one final act to play out?

Chapter 23:

The Aftermath

The Hall stood eerily silent, its heavy walls holding the weight of what had transpired. The once-grand dining room, where laughter and chatter had filled the air mere hours ago, was now a hollow shell of its former self. Shadows stretched lazily across the room, no longer writhing with malice but calm, as though the house itself was finally at peace.

Lady Phillips remained in the center of the room, her glowing eyes dimmed slightly. Her tall, spectral figure seemed to blend into the darkened space, her presence no longer oppressive but strangely serene. The icy chill that had gripped the Hall was lifting, replaced by a stillness that was neither warm nor cold—just empty.

The crumpled photograph of Olivia with Rachel and Greg lay on the floor, a quiet testament to the lives that had been torn apart. Near it, the faint scorch marks of Jamie, Bella, and Lucy's presence lingered like scars on the wooden floor. The Hall had seen its reckoning, and now it was simply... still.

Lady Phillips turned slowly, her gaze sweeping across the room as if she were ensuring every last piece of judgment had been delivered. But as she moved, a faint sound broke the silence—a creak from the upper floors, so soft it could have been the groan of the old house settling.

Her glowing eyes narrowed slightly, her head tilting as though she were listening. The sound came again, louder this time. Footsteps, slow and deliberate, descending the grand staircase.

Her expression remained neutral, but there was a flicker of something in her gaze—curiosity, perhaps, or recognition. She turned fully toward the doorway, waiting.

The footsteps stopped just out of view. The air in the room grew heavy once more, not with malice, but with an unspoken question. The Hall, it seemed, was not quite ready to let go of its final act.

From the shadows of the hallway, a faint figure emerged. It wasn't one of the victims; their judgments had been sealed, their fates final. This figure was different—faint and translucent, like a memory brought to life. It was a man, tall and broad-shouldered, his face lined with age and regret. He wore a suit that was decades out of fashion, its edges frayed as though it had been worn in life and beyond.

Lady Phillips' gaze softened slightly as the figure stepped closer. "Phillip," she said quietly.

The man—Phillip—paused, his expression solemn. "Eleanor," he replied, his voice deep and resonant despite its ghostly quality. "It's over, then?"

Lady Phillips—Eleanor—nodded slowly. "It is done. The Hall has seen justice. The sins have been accounted for."

Phillip's gaze drifted around the room, lingering on the scorch marks and the faint remnants of the lives that had been judged. "And what of you? Is your task complete?"

Eleanor's glowing eyes dimmed further, her tall form seeming to shrink slightly. "It is... for now. The Hall will rest, as will I. But if the sins return, so shall I."

Phillip nodded, his expression pained. "And what of the living? Will they ever truly leave this place?"

Eleanor tilted her head, her gaze thoughtful. "The Hall holds their secrets now. Those who trespass here will feel its weight, its whispers. But they will not be judged unless their sins demand it."

As the conversation faded into silence, the Hall itself seemed to sigh. The flickering candles steadied, their flames burning with a warm, golden glow that had been absent for decades. The shadows receded further, pulling back into the corners of the room as though retreating to sleep.

Eleanor turned to Phillip, her gaze softening. "You stayed," she said quietly. "Even after all this time."

"I could not leave," Phillip replied. "Not while you were bound here. Not while your work remained unfinished."

Eleanor's faint smile was the closest thing to warmth the Hall had seen in years. "Then let us both rest."

Phillip offered his arm, and Eleanor hesitated for a moment before taking it. Together, they began to fade, their forms blending into the soft glow of the Hall's light. As they disappeared, the oppressive weight that had hung over Windemere Hall for decades lifted entirely.

The Hall was silent once more, but it no longer felt haunted. It felt empty, yes, but not unkind. The scars of judgment would remain, but the House itself seemed ready to move forward, its restless history finally laid to rest.

Outside, the storm that had raged all night had subsided. The moon shone brightly above Windermere Hall, its pale light casting long shadows across the grounds. The once foreboding silhouette of the house now seemed almost tranquil, its dark windows reflecting the silver glow of the night sky.

But deep within the Hall, somewhere in its labyrinth of rooms and corridors, a faint whisper echoed. It was soft, almost imperceptible, but it lingered just long enough to remind the world that Windermere Hall was not entirely silent not yet !.

Epilogue:

The Hall's Next Chapter

Windermere Hall stood silent under the pale light of dawn, its once-foreboding presence softened by the glow of a new day. The storm had passed, and the grounds were drenched with rain, the air heavy with the scent of wet earth. From the outside, the Hall looked like any other grand, historic estate—beautiful, timeless, serene. But for those who knew its history, Windermere Hall was anything but ordinary.

Inside, the house was still. The faint scorch marks on the dining room floor, the shattered glass, and the echoes of the night's terror had all vanished, as if the Hall itself had erased the evidence of what had occurred. Yet the energy of the place remained, waiting, watching. The Hall had been satisfied, but its hunger for justice could never truly be quenched.

The Inheritance

In a quiet office miles away, a solicitor sat at his desk, pouring over a stack of papers. His eyes lingered on the most recent entry in his file—the official declaration of Jamie Phillips' death. The heirs of Windermere Hall were few and far between now, the once-proud family line all but extinguished.

After Jamie's demise, the title of Windermere Hall had passed, by default, to a distant relative: a young woman named Charlotte Whitmore. She was twenty-eight, a freelance artist living in a London flat she could barely afford. She'd never heard of Windermere Hall until the letter arrived— a formal, weighty document informing her that she was now the owner of an estate she'd never visited, tied to a family she barely knew.

A New Arrival

Several weeks later, Charlotte stood at the wrought iron gates of Windermere Hall, her suitcase in hand and her expression a mix of awe and apprehension. The grandeur of the house took her breath away, its towering spires and intricate stonework whispering of wealth and power from another time. Yet something about it felt... off. The windows, dark and reflective, seemed to watch her as she hesitated at the gates.

"This is mine now," she murmured to herself, her voice trembling slightly. "This... this is home." The gates creaked open slowly, almost as if they had been expecting her. Charlotte stepped onto the gravel drive, her footsteps crunching loudly in the quiet. The air felt colder here, heavier, though she told herself it was just the lingering chill of autumn.

As she approached the front door, it swung open on its own, revealing the grand foyer beyond. The air inside was still and cool, carrying a faint, inexplicable scent of lavender and something older, earthier.

"Hello?" Charlotte called out, her voice echoing through the cavernous space. There was no answer, but the Hall seemed to respond in other ways—a subtle shift in the air, a faint creak from the upper floors. Charlotte shivered, but she shook it off, stepping inside and closing the door behind her.

The Hall Waits

Charlotte wandered through the Hall, her footsteps echoing softly on the polished floors. Dust motes floated in the weak sunlight that filtered through the tall windows, casting long, golden beams across the room. The house was magnificent, its beauty undeniable, but there was a weight to it—an invisible pressure that seemed to follow her as she explored.

In the dining room, she paused, her eyes drawn to the faint outline of a scorch mark on the floor. She crouched down, running her fingers over the wood, but the mark was cold, lifeless, as though it had been there for centuries.

"Strange," she muttered, standing and dusting off her hands.

As Charlotte moved deeper into the Hall, she couldn't shake the feeling that she wasn't alone. The air seemed to hum faintly, the shadows on the walls shifting ever so slightly. She told herself it was just her imagination—after all, she'd been warned about the Hall's long history, its many myths and legends.

"Just a house," she said to herself, her voice breaking the heavy silence. "Just an old house."

But as she turned down a long corridor, a faint whisper carried through the air, stopping her in her tracks. It was soft, barely audible, but unmistakable.

"Charlotte..."

Her heart leapt into her throat as she spun around, her wide eyes searching the empty hallway. There was no one there. The house was silent once more, as though the whisper had never existed.

A Legacy of Secrets

Charlotte shook her head, laughing nervously to herself. "Get a grip," she muttered, forcing her feet to move forward. "It's just an old house settling. Nothing to worry about."

But the Hall had other plans.

As Charlotte continued to explore, she passed by a tall mirror in the grand hallway. For a brief moment, as she glanced at her reflection, she could have sworn she saw someone standing behind her—a tall woman in a gray gown, her eyes glowing faintly.

When she whipped around, the hallway was empty. But the faint scent of lavender lingered in the air.

A New Chapter Begins

Windermere Hall had a new mistress now, a new life to entangle in its web of secrets and judgment. Charlotte had no idea what awaited her within its walls, no idea of the history that had unfolded in the very rooms she now called home. But the Hall knew. The Hall always knew.

As night fell over the estate, the shadows lengthened, and the house settled into a familiar rhythm. The whispers began again—soft, indistinct, but full of promise. Windermere Hall had claimed many lives, but it was far from finished.

After all, every house needs a purpose.

The End

For now anyway !!!!

Other Books available on amazon by Karl Hartey

Lady Phillips Series
Judgement at Windermere Hall Book one

Financial & Personal Development Books
Smart Money Series

1. **Smart Money: How to Create Financial Freedom**
2. **Smart Money: Retirement Made Simple**
3. **Smart Money: Securing Your Legacy**
4. **Smart Money: Tax Efficiency for High Earners**
5. **Smart Money: Investing with Confidence**

Other Financial Books

6. **How to Survive the Sharks** – Insider knowledge on the financial services industry.
7. **All You Need to Know About Retirement** – Insights into retirement and pension planning.
8. **All You Need to Know About Divorce and Financial Settlements** – Navigating divorce and financial settlements.

9. **All You Need to Know About Trusts** – Understanding the role and use of trusts.

10. **All You Need to Know About Investing** – A guide to understanding investments.
11. **Securing Your Family's Financial Future: 60 Top Tips** – Practical advice for financial security.
12. **All You Need to Know About Inheritance Tax and Estate Planning** – Resourceful guide on estate planning and tax.

Gumball Rally Adventures

1. **3000 Miles: Our First Gumball Rally**
2. **Gumball 3000: Miami to Ibiza**
3. **Gumball 3000: Dublin to Bucharest** 4. **Gumball 3000: Riga to Mykonos**

Mollie and Tobie Series *Cornish Tails Series*

1. **Mollie and Tobie: Cornish Tails**
2. **Mollie and Tobie: Cornish Tails 2**
3. **Mollie and Tobie: Cornish Tails 3**
4. **Mollie and Tobie: Cornish Tails 4**

5. **Mollie and Tobie: Cornish Tails**
   5 (Famous Dog Walks in Cornwall)

Other Adventures

6. **Mollie and Tobie: Greek Tails**
7. **Mollie and Tobie: Shropshire Tails**
8. **Mollie and Tobie: Cheshire Tails**
9. **Mollie and Tobie: The Wrexham Wolfpack**
10. **Mollie and Tobie: Dubai Adventures**
11. **Mollie and Tobie: Saving Santa's Christmas**

Mysteries and Sci-Fi

12. **Mollie and Tobie: The Secret of the Haunted Hall**
13. **Mollie and Tobie: The Mystery of the Underground Maze**
14. **Mollie and Tobie: The Secret of the Ancient Forest**
15. **Mollie and Tobie: The Time Keeper's Legacy**
16. **Mollie and Tobie: The Lost City Beneath the Waves**
17. **Mollie and Tobie: The Galactic Guardians**
18. **Mollie and Tobie: The Clockmaker's Labyrinth**

19. **Mollie and Tobie: The Cursed Crown**
Seasonal Nature Walks Series

20. **Mollie and Tobie's Seasonal Nature Walks – Summer Walks**
21. **Mollie and Tobie's Seasonal Nature Walks – Fall Walks**

Animated Stories in Progress

22. **Mollie and Tobie's Welsh Tails: Climbing Snowdon Mountain**

Printed in Great Britain
by Amazon

57742948R00082